THE SEVENTH ANGEL

The Land of the Heavens

Danielle Mendez

PublishAmerica
Baltimore

ISBN: 1-4137-9296-0
PUBLISHED BY PUBLISHAMERICA, LLLP
www.publishamerica.com
Baltimore

To all my friends, family, and everyone that helped me make my dreams come true. Thanks for always being there for me. I will now and forever be grateful.

"A Hero"
By: Danielle Mendez

A hero is not because of the shield;
Nor how brave they are on the battlefield.
A hero is not because of fame;
Or looks for trouble like a game.
A hero looks out for others;
And doesn't chose himself over his sisters and brothers.
A hero can be praised or hated;
But they will stand strong and, from memories, they will
not be faded.
No one needs to be a hero with a sword, shield, or even
wealth;
You can be a hero just by being yourself.

~PROLOGUE~

"Create thyself a land of beauty. Give life, freedom, and, above all, peace." say my father.

I am but the youngest of the Angels. I am called Kirlana, named after my very mother. I am wise, so say the claim of my father. Wise and full of grace. And now my sisters and I shall create a world. I give the name Hermalie. The Land of the Heavens. And to thee, Hermalie, thou shall have life, freedom, and peace. Thou shall have everything thy King of Heaven needs. I pray onto him my eldest sister, Malenda, keeps her peace as I shall keep mine.

~CHAPTER 1
THE BEGINNING~

The beginning of the world was a mystery to most humans. But it all changed because of one brave warrior and a story that this world would never forget. This story begins with the Lord of the Heavens. He sent his six beautiful daughters on a mission to create a world. They were the called the Six Angels of Heaven.

Kirlana, the youngest of the Angels. She is more wise and powerful out of the six .The Lord of the Heavens placed her as the head angel of this new Earth. She created the land, it's trees, grass, sky, and ocean.

Zeles, Angel of Life. She created humans, Elves, Menellians, and many other creatures.

Afelle, Angel of Love. She brings desire to every heart with a life of peace and understanding.

Hesion, Angel of Faith. The creator of hope, religion, and culture.

Falari, Angel of Mercy. She brings conscious and an act of true kindness to prevent rise of hate.

And Malenda, Angel of Death and Chaos. The eldest of the daughters who wanted nothing but power.

Together they created the world of Hermalie. Life was born and the Lord was proud. But the world would soon fall to pieces.Malenda went to her father and begged him for Kirlana's place as Head of the Angels and the ruler of Hermalie. Her father thought that she was foolish and too thirsty for power. He denied her wishes. And, with that answer, Malenda created world disasters such as tornados and hurricanes to destroy the world. Kirlana, with disappointment in her eyes, sent her sister to the underworld where she couldn't do any harm to anyone or anything.

Malenda had more than a craving for power now but had a thirst for revenge. She raised an army of demons to destroy Hermalie. Once the world was gone, Malenda is free from Hell. The demons brought with them pain and suffering for Hermalie's people.

Malenda became stronger and Hermalie became weaker. So, Kirlana and the Angels made a sword that had the power to defeatMalenda and her army. The Sword of the Seventh Angel. She sent the sword to the world and only the chosen one can not only pick up the sword but have the strength and courage to save the world.

One hundred years after the creation of the Earth, the sword chose a warrior princess. She fought in many battles and never lost one. She was strong but she only cared for herself .She decided to fight Malenda's army for a higher reputation. For that she died in the battle against the demons.

Thirty-five years later the daughter of the king, ruler of the Bensen Palace, picked up the sword and became the new Seventh Angel.But, just like the warrior, her heart was only for herself. She cared of nothing but riches and being higher classed. It came to the time when she had to face the challenge of Malenda's army. But she was taken and beheaded. The sword laid on the ground, and was never touched by anyone again. Until two-thousand years later, when the real hero will step into place...

*   *   *

The pale-faced servant girl laid on her bed. She was sleeping, tossing and turning. There were visions of blood and monsters running through her head. She woke up from startling bangs at her attic door.

"Wake up, you lazy girl ! You have work to do and your sleeping in!!" yelled the woman on the other side of the door.

The girl quickly pushed back her ragged sheets, jumped out of the bed, and started combing her long brown hair.

"Yes, Aunt Mary," she said. "Forgive me, Aunt Mary."

Aunt Mary yelled back at her.

"I mean it, Arlene Leggora! If you are late for your

chores tomorrow, I will see that you will not have a single crumb of bread for days! Understood!?"

Arlene tried slipping on one of her shoes but tripped trying to do so. "Yes, Aunt Mary," she said rubbing her side.

Arlene Leggora is only twenty-two years old. Her mother and father mysteriously died when she was only a baby. (By what she was told.) Her rich relatives, Count Anthony Leggora and Countess Mary Leggora of Alexandrite, took her and made her their slave. Arlene lived in the attic of the mansion. The walls were terribly made, the cold air seeped through them easily, and the ceiling was quite large. The only things that Arlene kept in her bedroom were her "bed" made out of just one long board wood. It was very uncomfortable. Including to it was a regular pillow and two ragged sheets that were covered in patches and holes.

To the side of her bed was a stool with a candle for night reading. And only two windows were on a wall. Between them was a rope that stretched across and it touched both windows. Arlene kept her clean clothes hanging on the ropes. (She was lucky if they were kept clean.) The only friends that she had were the rats that came to the attic for a visit and the other slaves, Darwin and the twins William and Wilson Galind. The count and countess found them in the Black Woods and took them in as their slaves, as well.

Aunt Mary and Uncle Anthony sat at the table. Arlene, Darwin, and the twins served them their breakfast. Uncle Anthony was a handsome man. His black hair was always neat. He was tall and he was as pale as Arlene. Aunt Mary had the beauty of a princess for a woman in her late forties. Golden-blonde curly hair and sky blue eyes. She wore a silver pendent around her neck. The pendent was the symbol of the rich Leggora family.

Aunt Mary stared at Arlene, feeling much more higher comparing herself to her ragged-dressed niece.

"Arlene, child," Aunt Mary began.

Arlene looked at her, feeling really small like a crumb to a mouse.

"Yes, Aunt Mary?"

Aunt Mary took a sip of wine and began to talk.

"When my dear friend, Mr. Harless, arrives I expect you and the rest of you scums to run along away from our conversation this afternoon. We wish to speak to him in privet. Any eavesdropping and I will crack the whip! Is that clear?"

Arlene, still feeling small, said, "Yes."

Aunt Mary gave her a stern look.

"Yes, Aunt Mary!" she scolded.

Arlene jumped and answered, "Yes, Aunt Mary."

Darwin and the twins jumped as well. William almost dropped the plate of bread.

Uncle Anthony looked at Darwin.

"More wine, boy!" he ordered.

Darwin, nervously, poured him some wine.

"Yes, sir," he said.

Then Wilson set the bowl of hard boiled eggs on the table and William with the bread. William smoothed back his blonde hair. He tried to make it a little neat since he hated to be called 'scum'.

Aunt Mary looked at her four servants. She waved her hand in the air, telling them to go away. The four walked into the kitchen. Wilson put out the fire in the fireplace and the others cleaned up the mess that was on the table.

Time passed by quickly. Arlene dusted the knick-knacks of glass swans while the boys scrubbed the floors. Uncle Anthony wanted everything to be perfect before Mr. Harless arrived. But Arlene had no idea on why her aunt and uncle adored this man so much. What was so great about him? The afternoon came and the four servants met again in the kitchen to prepare the dinner.

Arlene looked at the boys. They were quiet and she cleared her throat in the silence.

"I had the same dream again."

Darwin stopped what he was doing.

"I'm not surprised, "he said." you have been having that same dream since we were little children."

William stepped in.

"I think your crazy, Love," he said. "You have dreams about war. A war with demons and other creatures. I think that the countess is working you too hard. Now you want to do something bad to her. You're dreaming about murder and that is what you want to do, Love. You want to kill your aunt and uncle."

Arlene rolled her eyes and wrapped some bread in a cloth.

"No matter what, William," she put the wrapped bread in the cupboard. "I'd never murder…"

Arlene was interrupted by a knock at the front door. They could hear the door swing open and the delightful distant sound of Uncle Anthony.

"Mr. Harless!" he said from far away. "How nice to see you."

The servants heard the chuckle of the old man.

"Good afternoon, Count Leggora," he said. "It's so

wonderful to be here in your lovely home. And planning for your party tonight will be splendid."

Aunt Mary's voice came in after his.

"Please, come in. And we can talk about it."

William and Wilson looked at each other.

"Party?" they said together. The twins rushed to the kitchen door and fought each other for the key hole. Darwin whispered,

"You two? We are not suppose to eavesdrop…We will get more bloody scares on our backs."

William and Wilson didn't listen and continued to fight for the key hole. William won and Wilson listened from the bottom of the door.

Arlene and Darwin had gut feelings that this was going to lead to a penalty.

"Come along," said Wilson. "Come and listen."

With sighs, Arlene and Darwin pressed their ears against the door. The continued laughter went on in the other room.

"Oh, Mr. Harless." said Aunt Mary. "You're such a tease."

Uncle Anthony cleared his throat and poured Mr. Harless some wine.

"Continuing with the plan, "he said as he handed Mr. Harless the goblet. "We should invite every rich man and his wife in Alexandrite, hire the best musicians, and, maybe for more entertainment, you can show our guests some of your tricks, Mr. Harless."

"Now, Count Leggora," said Mr. Harless. "A warlock's magic should not be used for fun."

The four servants were shocked.

"A warlock?" whispered Darwin. "Your aunt and

uncle are friends with a warlock? Why didn't you tell me?"

Arlene, dumbfounded, looked back at Darwin.

"I didn't know, " she whispered.

William twitched his nose and began to breath in harshly.

"William...hold it..." whispered Darwin.

From the kitchen came a loud: "Aahhh Choo!" Wilson kicked William in the shin.

"You couldn't hold it in, could you!"

Mr. Harless looked at the direction of the noise.

"What was that?" he asked.

Aunt Mary and Uncle Anthony looked at the direction,too.

"I haven't a clue, "lied Aunt Mary. "but I think I should check."

Aunt Mary stood up and smiled at the warlock. But, as she walked to the kitchen, her cheerful smile turned into anger.

Panicking, the four tried running out the back door. Wilson kept hitting William in the back of the head. Just as Arlene opened the back door,the kitchen door swung open and then appeared the angry Aunt Mary.

"WHAT IS GOING ON HERE!!??" she yelled.

Darwin almost had a heart attack from her booming voice.

"What do you mean, my lady?" he asked.

"Don't play dumb with me, Darwin Galind!" she yelled again. "I know you little maggots were eavesdropping!"

Darwin nervously rubbed the back of his neck and started twirling some blonde hair around his finger.

"We were just petting the stray cat outside, Aunt Mary. Honest!"

Aunt Mary looked at the opened door but she didn't see a cat by their feet.

"YOU LIE!!" she yelled. "I don't see a cat!"

"But it left when William sneezed," said Wilson.

"It's true," said William. "I'm allergic to cats and I startled it when I sneezed."

Aunt Mary, with some suspicion, said: "Enough! The four of you, outside now! Brush and feed my horses!"

She pointed to the back door and they walked out.

Darwin fed one of the horses oats while Arlene brushed it's beautiful mane. William and Wilson took care of the second horse but the playful animal kept running away every time they tried to brush his brown hair.

Darwin began to pet the horse.

"What are we going to do when the count and countess are having their party?" he asked. "Do they want us to serve their guests?"

Arlene sighed, "No. We will be locked in our rooms, as usual. Oblivious to this world."

She got on top of the horse. She looked over at William and Wilson and giggled, because they were still trying to get the horse to stay still.

"I'm going to escape, Darwin," she said. "I'm going to explore Hermalie. I want to see the Elves. I want to meet Menellians."

She picked up a large stick that was propped up against the fence.

"I want to have an adventure. I want to go down in history." She raised the stick high into the air like a sword.

Darwin shook his head.

"I admire your enthusiasm, Arlene," said Darwin. "but servants tend to dream like that and it never comes true."

Arlene threw the stick to the ground and got off the horse. She stared at Darwin's brown eyes and didn't leave them.

"I don't believe that, Darwin," she said. "I don't believe that at all. Not one bit."

Without another word, she walked away.

Darwin sighed and looked over at his brothers. Wilson jumped onto the horse.

"Got ya, ya bugger!"

The horse kicked his hind legs up and down, trying to shake him off. Wilson held on as best as he could.

"Hey! Hey! Easy there!" he yelled. William rolled on the ground laughing and Darwin felt miserable about what Arlene said. Her voice rang through his ears.

"I don't believe that, Darwin. I don't believe that at all."

*   *   *

Later on Aunt Mary sent Arlene to buy oats and carrots for the horses. The streets of Alexandrite were filled with rich people, servants, and beggars. Arlene hated the streets. It was a place for the rich to meet up, greet each other, talk about how they made their next million, kick a beggar man's bowl of only copper coins, then go home. Arlene arrived at a shop and bought some oats and carrots. When she walked out the door a couple of rich boys, standing beside the door, pushed her over and knocked the food out of her hands. The oats and carrots spilled all over the street. The boys laughed and then ran away. There was nothing Arlene could do. She is just a servant and she didn't have the right to stick up for herself.

"Oh, dear child! Let me help you," said a woman in a black cloak.

The woman lifted her up off the ground.

"You wish to help me?" said Arlene in surprise.

"Of course I do," she said.

She snapped her finger and everyone froze in their place. Arlene looked at the streets and the only thing that she could hear was the wind.

"How did you…how did…" Arlene stuttered.

The woman waved her hand in the air. The oats and carrots were back in the bucket Arlene was carrying.

"Amazing!" said Arlene in awe. "I thank you, Miss Sorceress."

"Sorceress?" questioned the woman. "Child, I am no sorceress."

"Then how did you do that?"

"I am gifted with it. Born with it. Everyone in my family is born with a power."

She waved her hand and the streets were in motion again.

"I wish I could do that. I wish I had a power. It'd make me leave this place."

Arlene took a carrot and gave it to the woman.

"For you trouble, my lady."

"It was no trouble at all."

The woman accepted the carrot and started looking at it with an eyebrow raised.

"And what is this?"

"It's a carrot, my lady."

"Carrot? It looks like an orange warlock wand. Does it possess great power?"

Arlene laughed.

"Does your family eat carrots?"

The woman shook her head laughing.

"No, I guess the people of Alexandrite have a different kind of food style than we do."

"I see."

"But I wish to give it a try."

The woman put the carrot to her mouth, bit into it, and started chewing.

"This is wonderful!" she said. "I must say you have great
taste!"

"Well, umm, it's for the horses."

"What are horses?"

"Arlene!!" called Darwin's voice.

"Oh no! I have to go."

"Go, go, child!" said the woman.

Arlene turned to Darwin.

"I'll be there soon, Darwin!" she shouted.

Arlene turned back to where the woman was standing but then discovered that she was no longer standing there.

"How strange."

*　　*　　*

Down stairs, she could hear the cheer and laughter of the rich folk echoing off the stone walls and into her little room. The sound of the music was soothing and it made

her want to get up and dance. She wrote in her diary —-
~ November 12,Hermalie Age 1284 ~

Today is my aunt and uncle's wedding anniversary .I hear the wonderful music, and people congratulating them. I wish my birthday was like this. January 13th.I wish I could go to parties.

And with that last entry in her diary, she heard clings of pebbles being thrown at her window. She opened it and saw Darwin, William, and Wilson smiling and waving to her.

"What are you three doing?" She whispered but loud enough so they could hear her.

Wilson answered her." There is a slave party on the beach! You must come along!"

Arlene shook her head. "I can't. The count and counte...."

"Don't worry about them!" said Darwin.

"Yeah!" said William. "They are too distracted with their own party. Now come on!"

Arlene shook her head once more.

"I don't want to risk getting into trouble. We almost got killed when we were caught listening to the conversation this afternoon. Remember?"

"Fine then,Love, "said William. "You stay up there in your cold lonely attic. And we will go to the beach, get drunk, have a good time, and dance the night away without you. Have a nice night, Leggora."

The three men started walking away. Arlene quickly put on a clean brown dress and put her hair in a pony tail. She looked out the window.

"Wait! Wait for me!" she shouted.

Arlene looked down and it seemed like the ground was moving. Arlene's hands were shaking as she began to climb down the mansion wall.

"Fall!" yelled Darwin. "I'll catch you!"

Arlene hated heights. She was afraid to fall.

"Arlene! Fall!" shouted Darwin. Wilson shushed him.

Arlene let go and she was screaming as she was falling. Darwin kept his promise and caught her. The four walked on the cold grass until they got to the beach.

*   *   *

The slave party was fantastic! It had two large tables filled with food that the slaves stole from their masters. Meat, bread, cheese, fruits and vegetables. There were wooden flutes being played and drums giving the beat to the music.

The slaves danced around a big bonfire. Arlene grabbed Darwin and they danced with the other slaves. Many people were becoming excited. They started clapping and dancing exotic dances.

William and Wilson, who love to plan all sorts of pranks on anyone, took a basket of ice and stuck it down a man's pants. The man stood up, because of the shocking cold, and jumped around trying to get the ice out of his pants. William and Wilson laughed. The other slaves, thinking that it was a new dance, jumped around with the man and started cheering and clapping. A woman looked disgusted at William and Wilson.

"Twenty-five years old," she said to herself. "and they still act like children."

Arlene and Darwin, breathless, took a seat at one of

the tables and poured each other some wine in their goblets. Arlene chugged down her wine and laughed with excitement.

"You all were right," she said trying to catch her breath. "it was a good idea to come. But we have to make sure that we make it back on time before my aunt and uncle realize that we are gone."

Darwin drank some wine and answered her.

"Don't worry, remember? None of the others are. Our masters are going to be so drunk, they won't remember if they even had slaves."

Arlene laughed and poured herself some more wine.

"Everyone, listen up!" yelled a man by the name of Edwin Brown.

He stood up on one of the tables and the slaves looked up at him and wondered what he wanted to say.

"I hear talk that tonight is the nineteenth anniversary of the Count and Countess Leggora, and there they celebrate and here is our only night of freedom! I say we had enough! For many years we have been beaten by our masters and serve them for no cost but pain! Is that the way our lives should be?"

The crowd shouted, *"No!"* at this question.

Edwin spoke again, "Then I suggest that we fight for our freedom! Tonight! Destroy our masters and bring down every single Leggora! Who's with me?!"

The crowd screamed and cheered. Arlene dropped her goblet and the wine spilled all over her ragged dress. Darwin stood up on the table next to Edwin.

"You're all drunk and mad! You can't kill the Count and Countess Leggora of Alexandrite! They are allied with a warlock! You don't have a chance!"

Edwin pushed him off the table.

"Don't listen to him! There are no such thing as a warlock, y'all!!" he took a dagger from his pocket and held it in the air.

"For freedom! "he shouted.

The slaves roared with excitement and took sticks from the bon fire. And they all stormed to the Leggora castle.

Arlene sat there, scared to death. The three male slaves stood beside her.

"Arlene, listen to me, "said Darwin." You need to run. Get out of Alexandrite. They know that you are a Leggora. I'm afraid that soon they will kill you, too…Run!"

"Alone?"

"Meet us in the Black Woods.We'll run off somewhere far from here."

Arlene nodded. She hugged all three of them and ran to the woods. The farther she ran from the beach, the colder it got. From the distance, she could hear the screaming of the rich folk and the victory cheers from the slaves. Then they faded out and the air was colder. Arlene sat in a hollow tree of the Black Woods. There was the sound of owls hooting in the trees and getting ready to hunt for prey. Wolves howled at the moon. Arlene sat there trying to keep herself warm.

The Black Woods were gloomy. No birds, rabbits, or a deer. Only owls, wolves and other mysterious beings. Arlene looked up the hollow tree. The highest point was pitch dark and empty. She laid her head down and closed her eyes. Sleeping there was nothing different than in her attic. But, just as she was about to fall asleep, the vibration of large footsteps made the tree rattle.

'*The riot!!*' she thought. '*They must be looking for me!*'

She moved to the side of the tree and blended in well with the darkness.

The footsteps were closer and they stopped beside the tree. But it wasn't the sound of Humans. It was the sound of two different beings.

"What is it?" said one of the creatures.

He had an low evil voice that made her shake.

"I sense a mortal," said the other.

Arlene shivered from the cold and, also, being scared.

"Fresh meat! Finally, I'm starving! Let's search!"

The two creatures walked passed Arlene's hiding spot and she managed to get a glimpse of them.They were demons! They had red skin and dark eyes. They both gripped strange-looking swords with their claw-like fingers.

When they were out of sight, she decided to run for it. She walked out, turned the opposite direction, and stepped on a twig which made a loud CRACK! The monsters turned around and held their swords in the air.

"Stop, you!" They said at different times.

But Arlene didn't stop. She ran for her life as fast as she could. Until she tripped over a silver object sticking out of the ground.

~CHAPTER 2
THE CHOSEN ONE~

Arlene turned around and looked at the object that she tripped on. The object was buried but she took it out with one clean pull. It was a sword. The blade of the sword had no dirt or mud on it. She couldn't read the writing on the blade because it was in a different language. The handle was beautiful. Made of some type of white marble and engraved with gold angels. On the end of the handle, It looked like a small crystal ball.

She took her eyes off the sword and looked at her surroundings. More demons were arriving. The creatures looked at her and then at the sword.

"It's her!" said one of the demons. "She's the new chosen one!"

"Get her!"

They came closer and Arlene's heart raged in terror. She had no choice but to fight through them. With all the strength she had, she was swinging the sword at them. She didn't believe that she'd get one of them for it was mainly to keep them away from her, but she sliced one in the arm. The demon screamed and shoved her to the ground. The side of her head was cut when she landed on a root sticking out of the ground. The demon's sword began to thrust its way to her body but she moved just in time.

Arlene knew that she had no chance of survival. So she ran as fast as she could. The cold air was thick and she was losing her breath. Arlene thought that she lost them. But she found herself standing in front of a demon. He took her by the neck and began to squeeze as hard as he could. Arlene dropped the sword and tried to free her neck from his grasp. She was getting dizzy and she thought that she was going to die.

Then, just about when it seemed it was all over, a Centaur took his staff and hit the demon on the back of his head. He released the unconscious Arlene.

The Centaur was tall and muscular. His body was covered in short pearl-white hair. His skin on his upper body was a fair peach. His hair, short and red. The staff he held in his hand was long and silver.

Ignoring Arlene, the gang of monsters went to attack the Centaur. There was a continuous swish and clang of swords against the staff. The Centaur took down as many demons as he could. But one out of many was too much. The Centaur was struck in the arm with a large arrow. He held his arm and tried to keep the blood from dripping.

Out of the trees came, not one, but three Elves. Two males and one female. All dark haired and really tall. They were fierce fighters. Their silver swords flew across the monsters with no mercy. The screams of the demons were eerie. The Centaur looked at the Elves and decided to rest himself under the nearest tree.

"Retreat!!" yelled a demon. And all the monsters sprinted and disappeared with a red flash.

The Elves wiped the sweat from their foreheads and put their swords back into their sheaths. One of the male Elves hustled to the Centaur's side and examined the wounded arm.

"Oh, Evensen," said the Elf. "Why did you run off like that? You could have been killed."

Evensen pulled the arrow out of his arm and moaned in pain. The Elf took a cloth from his robe pocket and wrapped it around his wound.

"I had to, Rozin," said Evensen. "I had to save her."

He pointed at Arlene, who was still unconscious. Rozin walked over to her and put his fingers on her neck.

"She is still alive."

"Oh, poor dear," said the female Elf.

She walked over to Arlene and used her creamy white hand to push her hair away from her head injury. Rozin looked as well.

"She looks like a goddess," said the other Elf.

Rozin laughed.

"Indeed, Eron. But I think that she is just…"

Rozin paused and looked at Arlene's ears.

"A human! Leave her, Glorifia! We have no time to waste on mortals."

He walked away and helped Evensen off the ground.

"Leave her here to die? I shall not! I can take her with us where…"

"No, Gloria!" said Rozin. "Remember the last time that we helped a human? Our family was almost destroyed."

Eron looked at his brother.

"This is only a young girl, Rozin. She will not be like that backstabbing soldier we saved years ago."

"How do you know that?" hissed Rozin.

Evensen spoke up.

"I saw her take it."

The three Elves drew their attention to the Centaur.

"Take what?" said Gloria as she lifted Arlene.

"I saw her take the sword. Pulled it straight out of the ground, I tell you! She is the Seventh Angel. Chosen by the six angels themselves! I'm sure you know about the legend of the sword. It is as old as this world."

"I know how the legend is told, Evensen," said Rozin. "The last two chosen ones were weak. Only caring for themselves. If she is the next Seventh Angel, then she is just like them. Selfish and caring for her own flesh!"

Eron took Arlene from Gloria. Three unicorns pranced into the Black Woods and Eron carried Arlene to his unicorn.

"I think you are wrong, brother," he said.

Rozin turned to him and gave him a glare.

"Oh, am I? You are only two thousand one hundred and twenty years old! You are still young and naive!"

Eron sighed.

"There is something about this girl. I can feel it. She can't be like the others."

"You assume too much."

Rozin got on top of his white unicorn and rode off into the night and Evensen followed. And Eron followed behind Evensen, with Arlene. Gloria picked up Arlene's sword.

"The Sword of the Seventh Angel," she said to herself.

She kept it safe and rode off with the others. The four, with Arlene, escaped from the Black Woods onto Hermalie Field. The moon was bright and there were millions of stars in the sky. The air was still bitter cold but that didn't stop them from reaching their next destination. Lindolin City. Home of the Elves.

*   *   *

Once again, the visions of monsters appeared in her head. Arlene found herself standing on a battlefield. The bodies of humans, Elves and Menellians all over the place. Heads of demons oozed blood into the Earth. Arrows flew over her head and they hit the demons. She quickly ran for cover. As she was running, she stopped in front of a demon. Being careless, she ran her body into the blade. The sword pierced her heart.

Arlene screamed and sat up quickly in a bed. She looked around and found herself in a room painted with green and gold, a marble fireplace had a fire going, and the canopy that she was sleeping in was an elegant white. Then she saw seven Elf children looking at her.

"We must have woken her up when we were talking, I suspect," said one of the Elves.

"No, she must have had a bad dream."

"Is she a princess? I think she's pretty."

"I think she's a fairy. Not a princess."

"Don't be stupid! Then where are her wings?"

"Does she talk?"

A cute little Elf girl walked up to Arlene.

"Hello." she said." My name is Josephine. What is your name?"

"Umm....Arlene. Arlene Leggora."

"How old are you, Arlene."

"I'm....I'm twenty two."

The children started talking all at once.

"I'm one hundred and twenty two." said Josephine.

"I'm one hundred and eighteen."

"I'm one hundred and twenty four."

"I'm one hundred and thirty."

"Well today is me burfday!" said a small boy. "And me only one hun-ded 'n' twenty seven."

Gloria walked into the room. She had a white dress on and her black hair was in two long french braids. She eyed the children.

"Did you wake her up?" she asked.

"No, my lady. She had a nightmare."

"It's true. She moved around a lot and she was screaming."

"We thought that she'd like some company."

"It was scary, my lady. She was screaming like this..."The children started acting out Arlene's screaming. Gloria sat a tea kettle on a small table.

"Run along, all of you. You know better not to disturb a patient."

The children bowed and curtsied and ran out the door. Arlene felt the bandage on her head and then looked at Gloria.

"Who are you?" she asked. "Where am I?"

Gloria smiled and poured a hot liquid into a cup.

"You are in Lindolin City. I'm Glorifia Whitestone. You can call me Gloria."

She handed Arlene the cup.

"Drink this. It will help you relax."

Arlene took the cup and looked at Gloria's Elf ears.

"Lindolin City? Really? This is the greatest day of my life. I always wanted to meet an Elf."

She took a sip of the liquid. It tasted like peaches and strawberries.

"My older brothers, a Centaur, and I helped you on your time of need last night."

"Thank you," said Arlene.

Eron and Rozin walked into the room. Arlene looked at the Elf men and thought both of them were very handsome. Tall and both had black hair like their sister.

"These are my brothers," said Gloria. "Eron and Rozin Whitestone."

Arlene smiled at them.

"My name is Arlene Leggora. From the town of Alexandrite."

"Leggora? Are you a daughter of the Count and Countess of Alexandrite?" asked Eron.

She shook her head.

"No, I am the niece. I ran away because all the slaves started a riot and attacked the rich folk at the Count and Countess' wedding anniversary party."

The Elves' faces had a sense of sorrow. Arlene could tell.

"You managed to escape. You're lucky. Everyone was killed at Alexandrite." said Rozin.

Arlene's heart sank at this news. Her thoughts then dwelled on Darwin and the twins.

"Are you sure everyone was killed?"

"Except for one man. A warlock by the name of Sama Harless. He managed to escape the uncontrolled fire." answered Gloria.

Arlene felt low again and began to cry. Gloria tucked some hair behind her ear.

"Why, child. Why do you mourn?"

She still cried and buried her face in her hands.

"Darwin, William, and Wilson. They can't be dead. My only friends in this world."

Eron put his hand on her shoulder. Then he began to speak to his sister.

"Wait! The warlock was accompanied by others. I couldn't tell if they were male or female. But could it be Arlene's friends?"

Gloria answered: "I do not know, Eron. But it could have been other warlocks. From the reports of the Menellians, who were at the scene, no human could have survived that terror last night."

"No one knows that for a fact," said Eron. "I think Miss Leggora had the right to see for herself."

Eron extended his hand to Arlene.

"If you wish to see the warlock, come follow me."

They all walked down the pearl staircase and then outside. The elegant city was full of trees and beautiful flowers. Everything was in green, gold, and white. An absolutely breath-taking city bathed in beauty.

The sun was bright and it shined in the garden of the Whitestone Castle. There was the Centaur, Evensen, and the warlock, Sama Harless. And, not too far away from them, stood Darwin and the twins fishing for gold fish in the crystal blue pond.

Arlene cried tears of joy and ran through the garden to catch up with them.

"Darwin!"

Surprised, Darwin and the twins looked behind them

to spot Arlene.

"Arlene!" they yelled back all together.

They dropped their rods and ran to her. Darwin was the first to give Arlene a hug. William and Wilson each gave her a kiss on her pale colored cheeks.

Evensen and Sama smiled at this happy sight. Sama leaned into his wooden walking stick. He let the bright sun shine down on his old wrinkled face.

Rozin, Eron, and Gloria walked back into the Elf castle. Rozin had a look of despair. He feared that the downfall of his family and his people. He stared out into the city, as if the whole world would cease to exist.

Gloria and Eron walked beside their brother and looked out with him. Gloria spoke up in the silence.

"Eron, Miss Leggora will need some training. She has no knowledge on how to fight. Even the tale of the chosen one. The Seventh Ange…"

"This was a big mistake!" Interrupted Rozin. "Our home and our people will burn in the hands of Malenda. For what? Because you two put your faith in a Leggora that has never picked up a sword."

Eron shook his head. "Rozin, even tough the count and countess were known to be greedy and unkind, I find that Miss Leggora is different from her aunt and uncle. And Arlene has a heart of gold. I saw it when she saw her friends."

Rozin turned his head away from Eron in anger.

"Eron, you do not know anything about this girl! You do not know if the cold blood of a ruthless Leggora flows through her veins. Humans care for themselves. And show no kindness to others. They focus on reputation and wealth."

Eron closed his eyes and took a deep breath in and out. He was trying to calm himself and hoped to keep peace in this conversation.

"Do not linger in the past, brother," said Gloria. "True, the soldier that we saved years ago was not worth for saving. I know that when he sent in an army to kill us, our people, and steal our beloved treasures was a time of fear for all of us. And the last chosen ones were not heroines. But, today, we must take the faith that the angel, Hesion, has given us for this child. We have no choice. The sword chose Arlene."

Rozin walked over to the mounted Sword after Gloria finished. He took the sword off the wall and started reading the engravings on the blade:

"The Seventh Angel. A woman of bravery, loyalty, and the one that will save Hermalie. The Land of the Heavens."

He removed his focus from the sword to look at Eron and Gloria. They had curiosity in their brown eyes. Rozin gave them a half smile and tossed the sword Eron's way.

"You have my permission to train her," he said. "But there is a part of me that tells me that I cannot accept this idea. Not until I feel that the time is right."

Eron bowed his head but he thought of Rozin to be naive and ignorant. But he respected the thought that he didn't want his people to suffer.

*   *   *

After the dinning in the Elf palace, Eron took Arlene to the garden. The courtyard was decorated with all types of flowers. Eron removed the sword from the sheath and handed it to Arlene.

"I can't take this," she said. "I don't have any use for it."

Eron laughed.

"Of course you do. You are the chosen one. You found it and the sword is yours. Your destiny is now to be unleashed. Once I help you with your training."

Arlene looked down and dropped the sword.

"I don't want this burden, Eron.I don't want to fight."

Eron picked up the sword and gave it back to her.

"I know how you feel," he said gently. "Believe me. But if you are a woman that has a pure heart, think of this as a blessing and not a burden. I think you must know the tale. Come, sit down and I will tell you."

Arlene, with the sword in her hand, walked over to the wall where Eron sat himself. She looked at him and she was ready to hear the story. The Elf cleared his throat and began.

"You must know that the six heavenly angels created this world. All with a responsibility to make Hermalie the way that it is now. But there was one angel that wanted to make Hermalie her own. Malenda, the Angel of Death and Chaos.

"Malenda was not granted the world so she tried to destroy it. Kirlana, the youngest angel, sent her to Hell where she could not succeed in doing so. The other five angels thought that the world was safe until Malenda created Hell's Door. That is where the demons escape and try to do her dirty work.

"Not only are there the monsters of her underworld but Malenda got herself a witch. The witch's name is Raven. She lives in the Hell Castle in the Forbidden

Island. That is where Hell's Door is located, also."

"But what does this have to do with me?" Arlene asked.

"This is where you and the sword come in," he continued. "Kirlana and the other angels agreed to send that sword, in your hand, to our world. The one with the sword is destined to save Hermalie from Malenda and stop Raven from helping the evil angel from destroying our world. Hermalie is the Land of the Heavens and you, Arlene, are the Seventh Angel."

The servant girl rolled her eyes. "I'm not a hero. I've never done anything great in my life. What makes you think I'm going to save the world?"

The Elf answered back: "I'm not the only one. The angels think you can. No more talking. It's time for your training."

He pulled out his sword and waited for Arlene. She stood up, feeling a little nervous, and raised her sword.

"To begin the training, "Eron began ."You must start off in dueling position. Since we are both right-handed, we must put our left hands behind us."

Arlene followed directions and put her left hand, not too far out, behind her. Eron continued with the lesson.

"Now our blades come out in front of us. And we spread our feet apart like so."

He made the position and the side of his body was facing her. His sword in the position that he was describing. Arlene obeyed and did the same thing he did.

The training continued. There was slow clangs from the blades of the swords and they begin to crescendo every time they got faster. Eron also taught her how to use the sword as a shield from flying daggers and arrows.

The blade was incredibly strong. The daggers and arrows Eron shot at her seemed to repel perfectly. Arlene practiced day and night with

Eron every chance she had. She also learned how to bow on the back of a unicorn. It didn't turn out well at first because she accidentally killed one of the sheep on the Elf faming lands. The unicorn was going way too fast, she claimed, and it made the arrow turn. And it stabbed the poor sheep through the heart. William and Wilson learned how to throw daggers and Darwin was talented with an axe. And the more time Arlene spent with Eron the more she became quite fond of him.

~CHAPTER 3
MY CHILDHOOD
MEMORIES~

The grass in Hermalie Field danced as the wind blew upon them. The sky was ocean blue and the clouds were as white as snow. But there was something that was different from the rest of the world. One island that was so dangerous not even the bravest human or Elf would set one toe on the dirt. The Forbidden Island. It was always dark and gloomy. The clouds were not white, but black .And the sky appeared red.

Demons and Gargoyles surrounded the island. And on this island stood a stone castle. The castle was as dark as the island. It would give anyone chills down their spines. You would think that the Devil lived here. But there wasn't. The evil witch, Raven Darkshadow, lived here. Long black hair and wore a robe of crimson. Her nails were like cat claws and her hands were pale and her bones stuck out of them.

She stood in the middle of a room lit with black candles. A cauldron was beside her boiling blue and purple. She chanted holding a bat in her right hand. And, in her left, was a dagger. The bat tried to struggle out of the witch's grasp. But her cat-claws were digging into it's skin. It made it painful for it to move.

Raven stabbed the bat through the stomach. Blood oozed from the body and into the cauldron. It turned the bubbling liquid as red as the island sky.

A boy, no older than twenty one, walked into the room. His black cloak floated behind him. His hair was a dark as the witches and it was shoulder length. He was very tall and very strong. In his hand he held a chain. On the other end of the chain was an old man being dragged by the boy like a dog. Raven turned to his direction and smiled a cold vicious smile.

"Why, Xander my son. You brought me a sacrifice."

Xander's smile was as evil as his mothers and he looked down at the petrified old man. He shook in fear.

"I found him in the Bensen Forest," he said proudly. "I searched into him. This human has a pure heart. I knew he'd be perfect."

Raven took the chain from Xander and started dragging the old man. The man grabbed onto his neck and gasped for air. The witch held out her hand and a bottle floated off the nearest shelf. She grabbed it, took out the cork with her long nail, and held it to the cauldron. The potion flew through the air and into the bottle. Once it was all in, the bottle began to glow a blood red. Lightning strikes and the candles flickered. The bottle was raised in the witch's hand to a statue of Malenda, Angel of Death and Chaos.

"Malenda!" shouted Raven over the lightning and the wind. "I give you a sacrifice to prove my loyalty!"

The old man begged for mercy but Xander walked over and pried the old man's mouth open. Raven shoved the bottle into his mouth and he started to cough as the potion dripped down in his throat. The old man started turning white as he tried to get air.

"Let me make this a little easier on you."

Raven kicked the cauldron away from the fire and threw him into the flames. The man's flesh burned right off his bones. The flames went out and the skeleton laid there until it turned to dust.

"My lady! My lady?" called a demon.

"And what do you want?"

"Forgive me, my lady. But the gargoyles and the demons beg for the human."

"What for?!"

"We haven't eaten in days, my lady. A bit of flesh is what we need."

"You are too late. My sacrifice is done."

"But, my lady, we have no food no more."

Raven held her fingertips to the demon and flashes of red lightning shot into his body. He took in his last breath and exploded. Raven put the bottle back on the shelf and looked out the window. Xander stood behind her.

"What is on your mind?" he asked

"My mind is always on revenge, Xander. The Menellians will pay for having me banished from Hermalie. And, soon enough, their city will be mine."

The Island crawled with demons and gargoyles. It was never resting. Beside the castle laid a huge gap on the land. Hundreds of monsters jumped out of it and ran through the island. By Hell's Castle, laid there like an earthquake struck, was Hell's Door. Beside the gap was a red stone and magic swirled inside of it.

*　　*　　*

The night was cold again. Arlene tossed and turned in her bed. Once again, she seen more of the battle. It was raining. Blood flowed in the mud. She found herself between two armies. On one side were all the monsters. On the other side were the people of Hermalie. They were on the top of unicorns and they were in heavy armor. But there was someone that she never seen before in her dreams. A woman held up the Sword of the Seventh Angel.

"Charge!" she yelled.

Then the two armies began to clash into each other. And there was Arlene, standing between them. She screamed and ducked to protect herself. Then, right as the two armies were about to battle, she sat up in her bed quickly and looked around. She was still in her room. She was still in Lindolin City. Darwin, Gloria, and Eron rushed into the room.

"Arlene, are you ok?" asked Darwin as he touched her arm.

Gloria carried with her a tea kettle and poured some of the hot liquid into a cup, then handed it to Arlene. Arlene spoke quickly as the cup was handed to her.

"It's happening again. The same dream over and over again. A dream that I kept on having since I was five. It never goes away."

Gloria put her hand on the side of Arlene's face.

"Shh. Calm down, child. And drink this."

Arlene looked down at the cup that was in her hands and began to drink the hot liquid. The taste of strawberries and peaches lingered on her lips and she felt herself calm down. Eron was concerned about her dream.

"What do you mean you had this dream since you were five?"

"What is it about?" asked Gloria.

Just then Rozin and Sama Harless walked in. Arlene began to talk.

"I always dream that I am on a battlefield. It's dark and cold. Humans, Elves, Menellians, and monsters lay dead on the ground. I am standing there as if I am invisible. And they are fighting. And they are dieing."

Rozin and Sama looked at each other. Arlene took another sip and enjoyed the taste and the warmth.

"Eron, Gloria, Sama, meet me in the great hall. Everyone else go back to sleep."

They walked out of the room and allowed Arlene to drift back to sleep. Darwin walked away from the Elves and the warlock. The four walked into the great hall and took a seat by one another. Eron was the first to speak.

"This is unhealthy for Arlene. A dream of war can lead to danger. A human's mind wont be able to take such pain and make them go mad. It's fear in her eyes, I saw."

Sama cleared his throat.

"True, Eron," he said. "but I think that there is more to Arlene's story than just the fear."

"Mr. Sama Harless is right," said Rozin. "a human does not just dream of a night of war. Especially if it is a dream that repeats itself. She said it herself. Ever since she was a child, the same dream occured. A bloody battle of monsters. Good verses evil. I think that she is cursed."

"Who can curse her, Rozin?" broke in Eron."If Arlene were to be cursed, Raven would know who the Seventh Angel is. Only the angels of Heaven hold the secret. Malenda had no clue, unless she is told by Raven. Raven wouldn't have known when Arlene was five."

Gloria spoke her mind to the men.

"This could be a new for humans. I am not sure. But, for this, we must turn to the Menellians. At dawn, the day after tomorrow, we will head to Menellia. If anyone in this world knows about the powers of the mind, they do."

Darwin poked his head through the door.

"Please, tell me," he begged. "I want to know what is going on with Arlene. I've known her since my parents died and when her aunt and uncle took my brothers and I in. And, every night, I heard her scream. I want to help. Please."

Darwin shut the door behind him and Sama walked over to put his hand on his shoulder.

"We are not sure, lad. We will soon figure out what is behind Arlene's dreams. I promise you."

Darwin looked down at his feet.

"When I was a little one, I always thought that the Countess Leggora was whipping poor Arlene at night. When things like that happened, I couldn't do anything. I couldn't stop the blood leaking from her shoulder. But this was different. She screamed because of a dream. She becomes frightened and she cannot sleep at night. Her heart jumps. Sweat flows from her face. And there was nothing I could do…'til now."

Gloria gave him a half smile.

"No more worries, Sir Galind. The Menellians will know what to do. For now, you must relax and go back to sleep. Be strong for Arlene and things will get better."

Darwin nodded and bid everyone good night. Rozin looked into the fire in the fireplace and Eron looked at him.

"Are you finally warming up to her?" he asked. "You want to help her all of a sudden."

Rozin sighed and still looked into the fire.

"I let fear take over myself, Eron. And I worry for the safety of our people."

Rozin took his eyes off the fire and stared at Eron.

"I also fear for the safety of what we have left in our family. Nothing else comes first in my immortal life. It seems that the angels have shown me the light. It's time, my brother, not to fear but to save our world. I'll give Arlene a chance. We all need peace in Hermalie. That is what the Lord of the Heavens wanted for us. And the angels are more wise than I will ever be. I'll let time tell, for now."

*   *   *

The morning warmed the cold air. The bright sun shined down on the city. Everything seemed perfect as usual. Arlene sat by a unicorn and ran her fingers through it's long white mane. The unicorn laid it's head on her lap and enjoyed it's head being stroked. Eron walked out of the palace and decided to join Arlene.

"Good morning, Arlene."

She smiled at his greeting.

"Good morning, Prince Eron."

"Please, call me Eron."

"If that is what you wish, Prince Eron...er...I mean Eron...I am very sorry for disturbing you all last night. I will try my best to make sure that it never happens again."

Eron raised his hand in front of her.

"Do not worry about it. It's a good thing that you did," he said in a gentle tone." We are taking you to Menellia. The City of the Menellians. The queen is a wise woman. She will let you know what is going on with your childhood dream."

He stopped talking and started to stroke the head of the unicorn. Then went back to saying what was on his mind. This time Eron began to ponder out loud.

"I don't understand how humans can have these sort of visions. That has to be a really rare gift for your race."

Arlene looked down and the grass with depression. Then she started picking at the blades of grass.

"What if the Menellian queen doesn't know what is wrong with me?" she asked. "Or what if no one can figure it out?"

The Elf shook his head.

"You cannot assume everything, love. You went through the hard times as a slave. And you are letting yourself down with this negative attitude. Now you have to put the past behind you. If it has anything to do with you being our new Angel, and once you have learned to control your thoughts, think about all the good things that you can do. All the lives in Hermalie that you will save. One person can change the hearts of millions."

Arlene began to wipe the grass from her hands.

"That is the thing, Eron. I'm only one person. Just a girl in a ragged dress."

"Do you want to know what I think?"

"What?"

"I think that you, Arlene Leggora, are a hero dieing to spread your wings. You're just clawing out of your cage and you are ready to bring back the joy to Hermalie that was lost so many years ago. Trust me. I know. I'm two-thousand one-hundred and twenty years old. I maybe young but I've seen how this world has been."

Arlene raised an eyebrow. The unicorn lifted itself from the ground.

"Want to go for a ride?" he asked. "Let's get out of here and have some fun out on Hermalie Field."

Arlene bit her bottom lip in nervousness.

"I don't know. What about the monsters? Should we bring protection?"

Eron laughed

"No. We don't have to worry about that. The demons only come out at night. If they are exposed to the sun they will turn to stone."

Arlene felt a little safer after hearing him say that. Eron jumped on the back of the unicorn and made some room in front of him for Arlene. Arlene jumped onto the unicorn with the help from the Elf. She grabbed tightly onto the mane and the unicorn wasn't uncomfortable from the grasp. Since Arlene had the fear of heights she was afraid of falling off once the unicorn started galloping. Eron held her by her waist which made her feel more secure. The unicorn moved swiftly. The air was a little cold on the November day. Hermalie Field was green with some frost sprinkled on the grass. Arlene took the red ribbon out of her hair and let the breeze fly into her face. Eron smelled the sweet aroma in her hair and Arlene never had a moment like this. It was the most happiest day of her life. The unicorn stopped and rested by the Hermalie River. Eron and Arlene sat by it and watched the little fairies hover over the water. Their wings were glowing all types of colors and it was such a romantic setting.

"I wish to know more about you, Eron," begged Arlene. "What is your family like?"

"My family?" asked Eron. "When I was just a little one my siblings and I had been raised by Evensen. My mother and father died in a battle with the Princess of the Bensen Palace. The princess was the last Seventh Angel before you. She was a very selfish woman. She called for help and my mother and father fought beside her. During the battle they were both seriously injured. If they were brought to a safer place they could have been cured and saved. But the princess looked down at them as they were suffering. And all she said to them was,'Thy bones shall rot on the ground. Thy grave shall be with the monsters. I care not for the Elves. Take the dirt nap.

"My mother died right after the princess spoke her ill words. My father was stabbed through his breast. He begged a demon to kill him. For he saw my mother's corps and lost his will to fight for his life."

"That is a terrible story," said Arlene.

"Yes it is," agreed Eron. "What about your mother and father?"

"I never knew them. They died....but I don't know how. I was an infant."

She looked out into the sky and realized it was almost

dark.

"Let's not sound so sad now. I want to have a nice time with you before the sun is set and the demons come out."

Eron nodded his head in agreement. Arlene smiled, moved a little closer to him, and watched the fairies splash each other with water. Arlene held out her hand to one of the fairies. The fairy landed on the palm of Arlene's hand and stared at her and Eron. The fairy began to dance with grace. It's wings began to glitter different colors. Green, blue, purple, then pink. Arlene giggled and Eron clapped for the little fairy. It put it's little arms behind it's back, crossed it's legs, and blushed. It flew up to Eron and kissed him on his right cheek.

She laughed and joined the other fairies hovering over the river.

"Pixie Fairies and very kind creatures." said Eron. "If you don't have a lot of friends, a fairy is worth ten.'

He looked down at the grass and picked a flower from the ground. It wasn't fully in bloom yet. Then he handed it to Arlene.

"For you, my lady."

The fairy that danced on her hand flew over to the flower and gave it a little gentle kiss. The flower then bloomed into a red rose. Arlene looked amazed and accepted the rose.

"Thank you. It's beautiful."

Eron smiled his handsome smile and caressed her cheek. "I think you're beautiful." he said.

Arlene looked at him in a way that she had never looked at anyone before. And also she never loved anyone like this before. Three little fairies, including Arlene's fairy, began to push Arlene into Eron. She fell onto his chest and he caught her. The fairies giggled. Eron brought her chin up and looked into her eyes. He leaned in and kissed her. It was passionate and the fairies giggled once more. They began to sprinkle fairy dust all over the place.

The sun was about to set and the two rode back to Lindolin City. When they arrived Eron jumped off the unicorn and helped Arlene down. William and Wilson were in the courtyard practicing their sword fighting. Rozin as their trainer.

"No, no, William." he said. "You cannot turn your back. Always stay focus on your opponent."

After that Rozin turned and saw Eron and Arlene. His eyes lit up with anger when he saw Eron give Arlene her kiss goodnight. Arlene walked into the castle and Rozin turned to the twins.

"We'll call it a night, men. Get some sleep."

"Why, Rozin." asked Wilson." We were just getting warmed up."

Rozin took their swords.

"Tomorrow morning we are heading to Menellia. It is a long journey and you need to re-gain your strength. More practice later."

William and Wilson nodded and walked back into the castle. With anger, Rozin walked over to Eron. Eron began to bring the unicorn to the stables. Rozin grabbed his arm.

"Must have been an interesting evening, I must say." he hissed with sarcasm.

Eron shrugged him off.

"It's none of your business." he hissed back and continued to walk. But Rozin grabbed him again.

"Have you lost your mind? An Elf does NOT fall in love with a human! It is unnatural! It's like a dragon falling in love with a deer!"

Eron shrugged him off again.

"I do not care!" he yelled. "All I know is that I love her and I do not care if she were to be a bird and I a snake."

"A RACE SHOULD STAY WITH THEIR OWN RACE, ERON!!! SHE BELONGS WITH THE HUMANS AND YOU TO THE ELVES!!! THAT IS THE WAY LIFE GOES AND THERE IS NOTHING THAT YOU CAN DO ABOUT IT!!!"

Eron didn't listen. He turned his back to his brother and walked to the stables. Rozin stormed into the castle. And Princess Glorifia stared down at them from her bedroom balcony with the tears in her eyes.

~CHAPTER 4
A SECRET REVEALED~

Eron and Rozin didn't talk to each other at all. Every morning the Elves would greet one another. Mornings, afternoon, and before they sleep. But the two didn't even meet eye- to-eye. It was as if they meant it to be that way. Gloria looked at her brothers with sorrow. Tradition is tradition. And not greeting family for the new day should be considered Elf sin. Up the stairs in the castle, two rooms down, William, Wilson, and Darwin were packing for their trip to Menellia. And they started singing :

"To Menellia, oh to Menellia, where we will help our friend.
Our Elf buddies say they know the destiny that will bring her sorrow to an end.
On the path is where we will tread; and the Menellian Mountains up ahead.
To the south, we will travel with our beloved friend.
That will bring her sorrow to an end."

One room down from theirs Arlene packed her needs for the trip. Sama stood beside the window with his sac on his shoulder.

"Sama, I have a question," she said while she packed some more belonging into her own sac. "That night, when Alexandrite was destroyed, what happened to my aunt and uncle?"

The warlock turned his attention to her.

"You wish to know about their dreadful fate that night?"

Arlene shrugged, gave him an awkward half smile and nodded. Sama cleared his throat and spoke.

"That night Mr. and Mrs. Leggora were just about to have their dance together. Until that slave riot broke out. They stormed your aunt and uncle's mansion and killed everyone in sight. Some of them were too drunk to even burn one rich man with their torches. So the rich folk tried to defend themselves by taking kitchen knives. Your aunt and uncle came to me and we tried to escape through the back door in the kitchen. But we were caught by the surviving slaves and a pack of them grabbed onto the count and countess. They were stabbed to death. Some held me back when I tried to save them. And they took my wand, as well.

"I fought my way out. After I ran out of the mansion I saw a careless slave burning the castle. He was pouring rum into the garden and then lighting it with his torch. He forgot that all his friends were still inside doing their dirty work. The fire spread out all over Alexandrite."

"So how did you find Darwin and the twins?" she asked.

"I ran to the beach. I tried my best to stay away from

the fire as best as I could. That's when I saw them. They were standing in the ocean looking at the smoke that rose in the air. I told them to make their way to the Black Forest but they were all too frightened to walk into it. But then I saw two Menellians put out the fire. They sucked water from the ocean with their swords and sprayed it all over Alexandrite. Menellians do not use wands or staffs for magic, by the way. Their weapons carry powers. After that I took Darwin and the twins here to Lindolin City. Here is the only safe place for surviving slaves."

Arlene closed her sac after Sama was done with the story.

"Well thank you, Sama. Thank you for saving my friends."

Sama chuckled

"You're welcome, Arlene. Now then, we must head down to the castle and meet up with Rozin and the others."

Arlene frowned.

"I think that Rozin hates me."

Sama raised an eyebrow.

"Now, now, Miss Leggora. I know that Rozin may seen a little touchy but I don't think that he hates you. It was his idea to bring you to Menellia."

Arlene then started twiddling her thumbs.

"Eron told me last night Rozin and himself got into an argument. It's because...well...er...Eron and I have...have..."

Sama was curious on what she had to say next. The expression on her face made him really concern on what was going on between her and the Elf prince.

"Yes, Miss Leggora? Have what?"

She took one deep breath in and the words came out," feelings for each other" when she let the air escape from her mouth. Sama nodded his head slowly up and down.

"Feelings…"he said. "I see now. A human and an Elf falling in love with each other? The angel, Afelle, works in ways even us warlocks can't figure out. Maybe we will never in another two thousand years."

He looked at the girl with a big grin on his wrinkled face and he shook his finger at her.

"Now remember this, Arlene. Love is very powerful. More powerful than there is spells in a spell book. Love is magic that two people make. No matter what the race is. Afelle, Angel of Love, gave the races this type of power so they would have a sense of belonging and a sense of caring for someone more than themselves. And also do not worry about Rozin hating you. Deep down he is a caring Elf. He loves his family and his people. He'd die for them before hurting them. But, in this case, the world is in great danger. And he is trying to make things better. For the feelings you and Eron have for each other, he is being over-protective. But trust me, my dear, when I say that he will accept the love and he won't seem so hateful. Just give him time and patience."

Arlene smiled because his words made her feel warm inside. She ran over, hugged him, and almost knocking him over.

"Oi in there!" called out William at the other end of the door. "We are just about to leave! Come!"

Arlene threw her sac over her shoulder and walked out the door with Sama following.

By the time the three made it to the outside of the castle Rozin was cleaning the blade of his sword. Eron (with his back turned) put his sac around him and then his sword in his sheath. Evensen sat by himself and hummed a soft tune to himself. Sama walked over and greeted him on the new day. Wilson and Darwin sat near the garden and chatted with the little Elf that had a birthday the first time Arlene arrived in Lindolin City.

"My ears are not weird-looking," argued Darwin.

"You don' have pointy 'urs like me. They are bery round. I tink they are fur-ney lookin'."

The boy started to laugh. Darwin and Wilson rolled their eyes and started to laugh in pleasure, also. Just then a little Elf man walked up to them.

"There you are, Rupert," he said to the little boy. "You know not to run off before your chores are done."

Wilson and Darwin stared down at the little man.

"Aren't Elves suppose to be as tall as humans?" asked Wilson

The little man crossed his arms and began to laugh at his question.

"So you've never heard of a Dwarf-Elf, eh?"

Wilson and Darwin shook their heads. The Dwarf-Elf laughed through his pointy nose and held his hand in front of Darwin.

"The name is Benjamin Goldfeather. Put 'er there, 'o chap."

Darwin bent forward and shook the Elf's little hand. Benjamin put his arm around Rupert.

"And I'm sure that you know my son, Rupert Goldfeather."

Rupert held out his hand to Wilson and mimicked his father.

"Put 'er there, 'o chap."

Wilson smiled and shook the little hand.

"I'm Wilson Galind. And this is my younger brother, Darwin Galind."

"Nice to meet you, Galinds. Heard from King Rozin of the Elves that you are all off the Menellia. Along side Prince Eron and Princess Glorifia."

"Have you ever been to Menellia?" asked Darwin.

Benjamin smiled gleefully, as usual, "O' course I have," he said. "Remember this, young Galind. The Menellians are mortal Elves that always wear black or red. I never knew why. But they do all sorts of witchcraft. They don't use magic staffs or wands. They use swords and daggers. All depends on their elements, or something like that. The elements are Earth, Air, Fire, and Water. Also, they are very much into the stars."

Wilson became very interested in learning about Menellians.

"What are their personality traits?"

"Just like humans, I guess. Some of them are good and some of them are not so friendly. The evil ones love a good competition. The good ones have a pure heart. Like the Elf. You can tell the good ones from the unfriendly."

"Poppy, I'm hungry," complained Rupert.

"Right then. I knew you would be. Breakfast first and then it is chore time."

He turned back to Wilson and Darwin.

"Fare thee well on your journey, 'o chaps!"

He took Rupert by the hand and they headed back home. Rupert turned around, still walking forward, and mimicked his father once again.

"Fare thee well on your 'erney, 'o chaps!"

Arlene and William joined the others as they were

waving the Dwarf-Elves farewell.

"I have all my things ready," said Arlene. "How about you two?"

William and Wilson showed off their sacs on their shoulders while Darwin slapped his which was propped up against the castle wall. Eron walked over and greeted the group for the new day. (He took Arlene's hand and kissed it.) Gloria was next.

"My lady," said Darwin and the twins as they bowed.

It was time that Eron wanted to show them their surprises. They followed him to the stables. In there were four new unicorns.

"Go ahead and pick one," said Eron smiling.

The unicorns were all pure white and they were all anxious as their brand new owners. Arlene picked out the one with the longest mane. Darwin picked out the one that was most lovable. Once he walked into the stall it walked over to him and nuzzled his arm. William and Wilson chose the last two.

"I think that I'll call her Ivory," said Darwin scratching the unicorns side.

William and Wilson looked at their unicorns.

"How about you two?" asked Eron

"I will call him Daggar," said William.

"And mine is named Henry. I've always liked that name."

"I think I will call her…. Nikita," said Arlene

"Great choice, I should say," agreed Eron.

*   *   *

The sun shined on the snow and it was eleven-thirty in the morning. All the travelers carried their weapons.

(Including Arlene with the Sword of the Seventh Angel.) It would be careless if they didn't bring any protection if ever they were ambushed during the journey. Can't assume everything will be alright. Rozin stood in front of a tall male elf. His hair was a light brown and his eyes were a nice shade of blue. His name is Trevis. And he has been a friend of the Whitestones for centuries.

"Please watch over the city for me, Trevis. If anything happens send a message to Menellia."

"Everything shall be well, my king," said Trevis. "fear not. For Lindolin City shall stay the way as you see it. Peaceful and unharmed."

Rozin said *"thank you"* in his native language and bid him good bye. The royal Elves, the humans, the warlock and Centaur were all saying good bye to all the Elves and Dwarf-Elves. The whole city waved at them.

*   *   *

The group headed south. Their unicorn's haste was as fast as the wind. As well as the Centaur. It took them an hour to get to the Menellian Mountains and it had a path that led straight to the city. The path took forever, for it seemed like that. And the unicorns weren't even tired nor hungry. The afternoon came and the riders needed a break. Darwin took out some bread and wine and the humans began to eat. Gloria had a drink of water while Eron ate some fruit. Rozin groomed his unicorn. Eron worked up his courage and felt ready to speak once again to him.

"Please, Rozin, "he begged. "we need to talk."

Rozin didn't look at him and he continued to groom the unicorn.

"There is nothing to talk about, "was all he said.

Eron sighed and he snatched the brush from him.

"Yes there is. You cannot be angry with me forever. I'm no longer a child and I know well from wrong and right. And I know where my heart belongs. I want you to be there for me. Like a supportive older brother. And not my enemy."

Rozin was silent. He looked up at the sun and it was setting fast.

"We need to continue on," he said to the others. "We are almost to Menellia. At nightfall Hermalie Field will be filled with Demons."

Eron sighed again and walked away but then Rozin grabbed onto his shoulder.

"Now listen to me, Eron," said Rozin softly. "I hate this. I do not support this idea one bit. But never will you be my enemy. You are now and forever my blood. I just pray to the angels you know what you are doing."

Eron nodded.

"Of course I know what I am doing. Life changes and so do the hearts of many."

And without another word slipping from his lips, Eron walked back to his unicorn. Rozin got onto his and led the way to Menellia.

The sun set and the moon was bright in the dark sky. The group was now in front of the Menellian Gate. It was tall and silver. Rozin moved forward on his unicorn and spoke in a tongue that Arlene could not understand. The gate swung open with eerie creaks in the hinges. The unicorns backed up and the gate was completely open. They peered in and started moving forward. The place was covered with black tress that bent over the path. The moon glowed as if it were their guide to the city.

"It reminds me of a graveyard in here," said Darwin a little spooked.

The path finally got them to the city. Menellia was built on one, big, thick, black tree and it stood in the middle of a circle of small, bent, black trees. The city had a Gothic style and was beautiful with dark elegance. Rozin paused and got off his unicorn.

"Wait here," he said to his companions. "I need to search for Queen Harmony and tell her of our arrival."

He walked off. The rest began to talk amongst themselves while Arlene, disobeying Rozin's orders, walked away from the group to explore the city.

"I feel as if I've been here before." she thought." It looks so familiar."

Eron turned to talk to Arlene but then discovered that she was no longer beside him.

"Arlene?" he called but there was no answer. "Arlene! Where are you?"

Arlene walked to the back of the city. There was a small open space, a small courtyard. A boy sat there all alone and he was singing a song as he was leaning up against a stone wall. His voice was rich and wonderful. He was pale-faced and his hair was as dark as the clothes he wore. He dressed in black from his neck to his toes. Tattooed to his wrist, he had the sign of Capricorn. Arlene hid behind a small tree and listened to him sing:

Beneath the wall of stone;
laid there an empty throne;
My lass, my love, my joy through pain;
Your soul was taken and I cry the rain.

I still smell the lavender in your hair;
Still feel your skin so fair;
Now you lay in your resting place;
And never will I see your face.
By your grave I sat a Lilly;
You're with the angels and I hope you still know me.

Arlene moved forward to get a better look at him but then a loud snap came from under her foot. The boy stood up and Arlene did, too.

"I'm sorry, "she said. "I didn't mean…"

"An outsider!" he cried.

He took his sword from his sheath and pointed it at Arlene.

"Who do you think you are?"she scolded.

"I'm the prince of Menellia," he answered. "and any terrorisors on the city are to be killed."

Arlene looked down at his sword and then back up at him.

"My companions are here for a reason!" she hissed. "We are not here to fight the Menellians."

He continued to point the tip at her.

"Oh, really?"

He pointed to her sword and then the tip was pointing at her again.

"You carry a weapon, my lady. Plan to assassinate my aunt, the queen?"

Arlene became impatient with him.

"You know nothing of me. I don't have time for this. I'm taking my leave!"

The boy thrust his blade at her then Arlene pulled out her sword and stopped him.

"That's it! I've had enough of you!"

The two went on with the sword fight. The boy was fast and he was more skilled with his blade than Arlene with hers. The swords echoed through the air which made Eron run to the scene. Arlene lost her balance and tripped over a huge rock. He looked down at her and held his sword over his head and he was ready to kill. Suddenly Eron pounced on him like a cat to it's prey. The boy dropped his dark sword and stared at Eron in fear. Eron held the sword to his throat.

"Is this how you greet travelers from Lindolin, boy!"

The boy took his eyes off the sword to look back at the angry Elf.

"Forgive me!" he cried. "it's my duty to protect the city."

"Who are you? So I can report your name to the queen for your foolish behavior!"

"I am Nicholas. Nicholas Leggora," the boy said. "I am the prince to Menellia and the nephew of the queen, Harmony Leggora."

Arlene gasped and didn't take her eyes off the prince, and Eron, dumbfounded, slowly moved the sword from Nicholas' neck. The others sprinted in, along side Rozin and a woman with flowing blonde hair. She looked as pale as the boy. She struck Arlene as vivid and beautiful. She wore a velvet black dress with gold trimmings. Her eyes were fixed upon Arlene and Arlene could see a tear fall from her dark eyes. Arlene stared at her, too, and she figured out who she was. It was the woman from the streets that helped her in Alexandrite. Nicholas walked over to Rozin and bowed.

"Forgive me, King Rozin of Lindolin. I didn't know of

your arrival with companions."

The woman walked next to Nicholas as she kept her eyes on Arlene.

"Nicholas, child," she said softly. "Do you know who this is?"

Nicholas looked at Arlene in confusion. Arlene felt all the eyes peering on her.

"I haven't a clue on who she is, Aunt Harmony."

Harmony then whispered into his ear.

"She is your double. Your twin. Arlene Leggora."

The Lindolin companions muttered to each other. Rozin nodded at Arlene as if he were saying, "It's true." And Arlene and Nicholas eyed one another. For the first time in twenty two years, Arlene got a glimpse at her real family.

~CHAPTER 5
THE TRUTH UNFOLDS~

The Menellian Castle was the tallest structure in the city. It was beautiful and elegant in it's gothic-like style and it left the travelers in awe. Once they walked inside, the castle was lit with thousands of candles. On the walls were portraits of the Angels. They looked beautiful in their paintings. Kirlana, Zeles, Afelle, Hesion, Falari, and Malenda. Malenda's painting was different from the others. She was clad in armor and she held a spear in her hand. Harmony had them seated. Evensen stood by Rozin and Harmony and Nicholas sat in the thrones in front of their guests. Harmony stared at Arlene and smiled.

"It has been so long since I saw you, Arlene. Twenty two years ago."

Arlene had nothing to say about that but all she did was smile back. It was strange to her that she was able to look upon other family members who actually cared for her.

"I remember you," she said. "you helped me in Alexandrite. I was the one who gave you the carrot."

"That was you?" Harmony smiled. "You know, I still kept the carrot."

Harmony waved her hand in the air and the carrot floated into Harmony's hand. The carrot still had the bite on the end but it was rotting from time.

"Umm, just to let you know, carrots do not last a long time."

"Oh, well, lets just have it around until time consumes it. It's a memory of when we were first acquainted from so many years."

The carrot floated back onto the shelf of books.

"I had no idea that I had other family," she admitted. "I've lived with my Aunt Mary and Uncle Anthony and they told me that there was no one left in the Leggoras."

Harmony looked disgusted at the negative line that passed through Arlene's lips.

"How ignorant of Anthony and his bitter wife. Not telling you about the family that you still had here in Menellia. Your brother, myself….it was foolish of me to hand you over to them. I thought that they could raise you knowing about us."

"I believe not, my lady." admitted Arlene.

Arlene thought to herself that there would be no possible way that Uncle Anthony would tell her anything. If she even dared to ask him a question in the past she would definitely get a smack across the back of the hand. Arlene remembered it perfectly back when she was thirteen years old. She worked up the courage to asked Uncle Anthony about her family. He was sitting by the fire and read one of his favorite books.

"Uncle Anthony?" questioned little Arlene.

Uncle Anthony turned from his book and glared at her.

"Are you finished cleaning the stable, girl!" he demanded.

Arlene nodded her head nervously.

"Yes, sir."

"So what do you want from me, girl!"

"I wish to ask you a question….about my mother and father…what were they like? Why did they leave me?"

"Are you ungrateful, girl!"

He rose from his seat and Arlene wished she could take back all her words.

"I give you a bedroom of your own, food to eat, and clothes on your back! I am doing better than what your mother and father would do to you! And you dare to question me about them?"

"I…I…," she stuttered.

"Never ask me about your parents again, girl! There is no one left from the Leggora family. Now for your disobedient behavior, lift up your hand NOW!!!"

"And that is when he whipped me for asking."

Arlene hid the scar on her right hand under her sleeve.

"You were a slave, child?" Harmony's heart began to feel heavy. "They took you in as a slave."

Harmony bowed her head in shame.

"I put my faith in my own brother. My faith that the angel, Hesion, had given me. I gave you to him so that you would be safe and little did I know that you were going through pain. He makes you his slave. Forgive me, child. I should have known. I know my own brother. He is selfish and unkind. I should have known."

Harmony hid her face in her hand. Arlene lifted herself from her chair and walked up to the queen.

"Oh, my Aunt Harmony," she said softly. "but why did you need to protect me? Why couldn't I have stayed here in Menellia with you and Nicholas?"

Harmony took her hand away from her eyes.

"It was such a dark time the day that you and Nicholas were born. You two were born here in Menellia right in this very castle. Your mother, Kathryn, was dieing while giving birth. I was there helping her deliver her wee ones. Nicholas was the first to be brought in this world. Then, soon after, you arrived. Your father, Daniel, was the Prince of Menellia. And he gave you your names. Arlene Kirsten and Nicholas Samuel.

"That night demons and other serpents of Hell trespassed on the Menellian land. They were killing my people. Anyone that came into their path. But most of all they wanted you, Arlene. I begged Anthony to take you to the human side of Hermalie and raise you there. He agreed and flew away on his broomstick with you in his arms.

"My armies defeated the trespassers. But sadly, I rushed back to the room where your mother laid. But…I only saw the bones of your dear mother and father."

"How did that happen?" asked Arlene.

"I do not know, child."

Arlene didn't question that even though she wish that Harmony would give her a straight answer.

"My guess is that it was black magic. Raven led the armies in to destroy you. I do not know why there was no mercy shown to your mother and father. Then again, a non-believe in the angel, Falari, will have no mercy in their heart nor soul."

Nicholas looked down at the ground after Harmony was done with the story.

"I will have my revenge...,"he whispered in anger.

Harmony turned to him.

"What have I taught you, Nick," she said in bitter anger. "A taste of revenge is an easy way to become evil."

Nick relaxed his eyes and nodded.

"Yes, Aunt Harmony. Forgive me, Aunt Harmony."

Arlene hated those words. Even though they were for Harmony it still reminded her about the very words she hated to say and she had been saying them for most of her life.

'Yes, Aunt Mary. Forgive me, Aunt Mary.'

"We came for help," came in Eron. "Arlene has a repeating nightmare. A nightmare about a war."

"Is this true, Arlene," asked Harmony.

"Yes," she answered." ever since I was really young. Every night that is what I see."

Nick rubbed his hands together and walked over to Arlene. He touched her face with his fingertips and then closed his eyes. The others watched him and wondered. Then he started breathing in and out harshly and he began to sweat and shake. He let out a scream, fell to the ground, and covered his head with his arms. The others looked at him as if they were spooked by a ghost and Rozin and Harmony helped him off the ground.

"What did you see?" asked Rozin.

Nick spoke with a trill in his voice.

"I saw...the war of Hermalie. On the Forbidden Island. It's the most horrible battle that I have ever seen."

His eyes slowly glided to Arlene.

"How can you possible live with something like this?"

Arlene shook her head and Harmony spoke in the silence.

"You have the gift of premonition, Arlene. So do I and so does Nick. Nick also has the power to read minds. By what Nick has just said, I am sure that Raven Darkshadow knows that the Seventh Angel is still alive and she plans an attack on Hermalie. She will stop for no one as long as Malenda has her controlled. Now it is time, Arlene, to unlock your destiny."

She took the Sword of the Seventh Angel from the sheath in Arlene's side and held it in front of her.

"You are not a slave. You are the Seventh Angel. More powerful than the last two. And the heart of a princess."

"I'm...a princess, Aunt Harmony?"

"Princess of the Menellians."

She placed the sword in Arlene's hand and Arlene felt the warmth of the handle. It felt as if the sword itself was trying to tell her that it was truly her destiny.

*   *   *

The dawn crept up the next morning. It was January second. The snow fell into Menellia gracefully. Arlene stepped onto the balcony to take a look at the city in daylight. Instead of having her hair in her usual pony tail, it was decorated with black roses and designed in an exquisite way. She wore a black velvet dress and it was the most beautiful dress that she ever laid her blue eyes on. Nick stood by her side and stretched. He leaned onto the railing and stared at the city.

"Surly things here look more lively in the morning,

"he said.

Arlene didn't say anything. She was feeling a little shy which she knew she had to get over. This is her family and there was no need to be shy anymore. She looked down at the people while they crowded the streets of the city.

"They are different from us, Nick," she said. "They have ears like Elves. And also you and Aunt Harmony are paler than I am."

"First of all, we are half Menellians. We mainly show the side of humans. As for your skin tone, you must have more of mother in you. Mother was a full human. Father was half Menellian, also. Even though he could have passed for a full blood."

"How do you know all this. They died before we got to know what they looked like."

"Aunt Harmony has told me everything about them. And I looked into her mind and I saw the one moment that Aunt Harmony held deep within her heart. I saw the day mother and father were wed."

"How did you get a chance to see that?"

"I was seven and I did it when Aunt Harmony was sleeping."

Arlene laughed. The two were silent for a while and they just stared at the city.

"I am sorry about your love," said Arlene.

Nick was confused.

"My love?"

"The girl that you were singing about yesterday. You lost her."

Nick began to laugh.

"No, no, Arlene. That is an old Menellian song, It was

about the Menellian prince long ago who lost his princess. He loved her so much that he wrote a song for her. He sang it at her funeral. They are buried together in the graveyard. He killed himself two days later after he wrote the song. It is a big part of Menellian history. The first tragic love of Menellia."

"How did she die, Nick?"

"She was very sick. No one knew what was wrong with her. But the medicine witches back then said that she suffered from losing her soul."

"Losing her soul?"

"Black magic. But they were said to be crazy old hags. So no one knows."

Nick took her by the hand.

"Come on. I will give you a tour of the city."

They walked out of the castle and onto the streets. While they were walking Nick told Arlene about they ancestral background.

"Our great, great, great grandfather invented the flying broomstick. It is a magnificent way for Menellian to get around here in Menellia. Oh yes! Do you see that old house over there?"

He pointed to a grotesque-looking house.

"Our great, great, great grandfather was born there. It is very old and no one has the heart to tear it down. The people loved our grandfather and they didn't want anyone to destroy the birth place of the greatest king in Menellian history. He was the first Leggora to take the throne."

They continued to walk until they came to a potion shop on the public square.

"Let's go in here. I need to get a potion that will get my

broomstick working again. I ran out of magic and, well, I almost broke every bone in my body after I fell onto the castle roof."

"Yikes!" shrieked Arlene.

They walked into the store and Nick patted her on the shoulder.

"You go ahead and look around while I find my potion."

Nick walked away and Arlene decided to do that. Look around and learn. The place had walls full of potions and books. It was a little dark and filled with spider webs. A little black spider dangled by the side of Arlene's ear. She wasn't afraid. It just reminded her about the spider that use to be in her attic room. She happened to keep that spider as a pet.

Angels rest the little creature. She walked around and read the labels on the spiral bottles. Healing Potion, Elixirs, Potion of Fire, and Potion of Ice. She walked on and looked on the shelves in the middle of the room. Then she heard the giggles of two girls from the other side of the shelf. She stared at them over the bottles. The girls looked no older or younger than her. One had many braids in her dark hair and she wore a dark blood-red dress. Her skin was white and her pointy ears poked out from all of the braids. She had the Scorpio sign on her wrists. The other was also as white as her and her pointy ears poked out of her long blonde hair. She dressed in black and she wore the Cancer sign on her wrists. They were looking at a pink bottle and kept on giggling. It was annoying Arlene.

"Trust me, Topenga," said the dark haired girl. "Once Austin gets a taste of this he'll be falling for me and leave that Maisy girl."

"I think it will work, Demetra. You're more prettier than Maisy."

Demetra pushed back her long braids with her hand and smiled conceitedly. She then stopped smiling and looked around with suspicion in her green eyes.

"What is it?" asked Topenga. "What can you sense?"

Demetra turned and saw Arlene eavesdropping. Arlene looked away and started walking.

As she was walking she heard: "It's Maisy! She was spying on us!"

Arlene walked faster and tried to look for Nick but then she suddenly couldn't move. Her feet felt as if they were frozen to the ground. She looked down and discovered that they WERE frozen to the ground. Demetra and Topenga came from around the corner behind her and Demetra had her hand out in front of her.

"I got you, Maisy!" she hissed. "I'll teach you not to spy on me!"

"Let me go!" shouted Arlene. "I'm not who you are looking for!"

Demetra and Topenga looked at Arlene's face.

"How do we know that you're not a friend of Maisy's?" demanded Topenga.

"I swear it," said Arlene. "This is all just one big misconception. I am with the travelers of Lindolin City. We arrived here last night."

Demetra and Topenga looked at each other and rolled their eyes.

"Whatever you say, girl!" said Topenga.

Arlene didn't like the sound of that. It seemed like she was still in Alexandrite. With one snap of Topenga's finger the ice that froze Arlene in her place was then engulfed in flames. The ice melted and the fire disappeared.

"Now get out of here before my mercy towards you fades!" snapped Demetra.

Arlene glared at her.

"You don't scare me!" Arlene snapped back.

"How about now?"

Demetra drew out her dagger. A black and blue ball started forming at the tip of it. It became larger as she held it over her ear.

"Say good night!"

As soon as she was about to hurtle the magic at Arlene, a flash of green light darted at Demetra. She flew backwards and went straight through the store window. Many Menellians on the streets gathered around and looked at the window and then at Demetra, who was now nursing her sore back. She flew back into the store, through the gap where the window once stood, and landed back on the floor. Nick lowered his sword.

"Demetra Onyx!" he scolded. "and Topenga Jade! If I see you trying to curse my sister again there will be no mercy coming from ME!"

Topenga helped Demetra off the floor and started helping her swipe the dirt of her red dress.

"Sister?" she said with a snotty tone. Still trying to take the dirt off her.

The shopkeeper came in. He looked at the shattered window and then at the four menaces.

"What's the big idear!? Comin' into me store and destroyin' it!!"

Outside the people on the streets looked inside to see

what was going on.

"Don't worry about it," said Nick.

With one wave of his hand the broken window was put back into place.

"Mark me words, all of ya!" he scolded again shaking his fat finger at them." Anymore of this and I report it to her majesty, the queen! Now leave!"

He pointed to the door. Demetra and Topenga ran out. Nick pulled out a black bag from his cloak and tossed it to the shopkeeper.

"Fifty gold pieces for the potion and twenty five for our trouble."

He took Arlene's hand and they left the shop.

*   *   *

That night Arlene sat with Eron and Gloria on the stone wall in the courtyard behind the city.

"I've learned a lot about Menellians today," said Arlene. She opened up a book and started looking through it, "it says here, Eron, since you were born on December third you are a Sagittarius. And you, Gloria, you were born April fourteenth. So you are an Aries."

"Menellians may believe that," said Gloria. "but we Elves do not. In our culture, Arlene, the study of magic is a sin."

Arlene went back to studying. She lifted the book off her lap and held it in front of her face. Her sleeves from her dress slid down her arms and revealed her new tattoos on her wrists.

"Ouch!" winced Eron. "Did that hurt?"

Arlene looked at the Capricorn signs.

"Not as much as you put it. They were gentle carving it into me. It hurt at first, but then it wasn't so bad. The marks will become darker. They used a special needle to do it."

Arlene went back to reading.

"Barbaric!" shrieked Gloria. "Our bodies were designed by the Angels, and they shouldn't be tampered with any type of needle."

Rozin joined them with two swords in his hand. He handed one to Eron.

"I was becoming bored, Eron, "smiled Rozin.

Eron understood what he was saying. He drew his sword from the sheath and Eron and Rozin dueled in the middle of the courtyard. Wilson and Darwin walked out and sat near Arlene and Gloria. Wilson was rooting for Rozin and Darwin for Eron. Nick joined them with two broomsticks in his hands. He handed one to Arlene.

"Aunt Harmony has asked me to give you some riding lessons."

Arlene sat the book down and agreed to learn how to fly.

'*Fly*?!' she thought. '*I hate heights!*'

Wilson and Darwin were becoming more excited every time the Elves' swords clashed into each other.

"That's it, Rozin! Get him in the o' smack-a-roo!" cheered Wilson.

Gloria gave him a look. She had no idea on what a 'smack-a-roo' means. Wilson saw her look and just shrugged.

"Twenty gold pieces are saying Eron will win, "said Darwin to Wilson.

"You're on!" said Wilson pulling a small sack from his

pants pocket.

Arlene mounted the broomstick after Nick mounted his.

"Now repeat after me, "he said.

He gripped onto the broom with his white hands.

"Ves!" he shouted and the broom flew into the air. He then hovered over the others.

"Now you try!" he shouted to Arlene.

Arlene looked up, took a deep breath in and out, and then shouted, "Ves!" The broomstick shot into the air like an arrow released from the bow. Arlene hovered beside Nick and hugged her broomstick tight. She was appalled by how far she was off the ground.

"Let me guess, "laughed Nick." You're afraid of heights."

Arlene, clutching the broomstick and looking down with sweaty hands and a racing heart, nodded her head. Gloria put her hands on the sides of her mouth and shouted, "Just relax, Arlene!"

It took a while for Arlene to get comfortable with the heights and the broomstick. All Nick could do for her is teach her how to fly in circles. William walked out with a broom in his hand. He got Darwin's attention first.

"You're not really going to try to fly that, are you?" he asked.

William looked at the broomstick and then back at Darwin.

"Why not? If Arlene can do it then why can't I?"

"Duh! You're not a Menellian!" said Wilson.

"Well just for some kicks and giggles I will fly it, "said William.

William got onto the broomstick and he gripped it

tight. The others were too distracted with what they were doing then to focus on William's mischief stunt. William closed his eyes.

"Fly, broomstick!" he shouted.

But nothing happened.

"Go, broomstick!" he shouted again but nothing happened.

"Abra Kadabra!"

"Hocus Pocus!"

"Giddy up!"

"STUPID BROOMSTICK! I COMMAND YOU TO FLY!!" but once again nothing happened.

Wilson and Darwin started snickering behind their hands.

"Well if you two are so smart then how do you make this thing go?"

Darwin said: "You have to say 'ves' to ge…"

All of a sudden the broomstick shot into the air and William let out a scream as it flew like an arrow. The others stopped what they were doing and looked up at him. The broomstick was out of control. Twists, turns, loop-de-loops, and many spins.

" H O W - D O - I - S T O P - T H I S - TTTTHHHIIINNNGGG!!!!!!!!!!"

He raced towards Arlene and Nick.

"William!" shouted Arlene. "Not this way!!"

"I DON'T KNOW HOW TO WORK THIS TTTHHHIIINNNGGG!!!!!"

Nick and Arlene were knocked off their brooms. They started to fall to the ground but then Nick held out his hand and they slowly and safely touched the ground. William's broom flew down to Rozin and Eron. Eron tried to move out of the way but the broom followed him. It smashed into Eron and it made him fly right into the stone wall.

"HELP ME!!" shouted William.

Sama ran into the scene and he held his wand up to William.

"Stop, broom!" he shouted.

The broomstick stopped in midair .And William sat on the broomstick stiffed with fear. The broomstick started to fall but then Nick held up his hand and William landed on the ground softly. They ran to him and Rozin and Gloria helped him up. William was breathing in and out as he looked at Darwin.

"You are going to be the death of me."

"Me?" argued Darwin. "I didn't make you take the broomstick, Will!"

"You shouldn't of taken the broom in the first place!" scolded Nick. "They are dangerous and it shouldn't be in the hands of a foolish human."

"Lighten up a bit, Nick," said Arlene. "Yes it was foolish of William to do that but he has always been the daredevil. William, just promise that you will never do it again."

"I swear to the Angels! I will never touch a broomstick again! They are meant for sweeping up dirt and not meant for flying! Who is the numb-skull idiot who invented a flying broomstick in the first place?"

"Our great, great, great grandfather," said Nick and Arlene together.

*   *   *

The night fell into the city. The moon was bright and the January snow fell gently onto Menellia. Arlene looked out her bedroom window and out into the streets. A group of musicians were playing sweet music under her window. Then she stood in the middle of her room and started dancing to the music. Eron stood by the door and watched her. Then he quietly walked into the room and held out his hand to her.

"May I have this dance, my lady," he said in his charming tone.

Arlene curtsied and took his hand. They got into their dancing positions and they both began to sway to the music. The candles in the room flickered and the curtains flowed with the wind. Outside Menellians were dancing to the music which was now being sung by a Menellian woman. When it ended Eron kissed Arlene on her cheek.

"It was a pleasure, Arlene," he said. "Sleep well tonight, princess."

He kissed her hand and walked out the door. Arlene felt her hand and then walked to the window. Another song began to play and the people continued to dance. Arlene could do nothing more than to smile at this scene.

~CHAPTER 6
THE BENSEN PALACE~

Hermalie didn't rest because the demons ran through the land and fed on the poor animals. Everyone was suppose to stay in doors after twelve o'clock. Not unless they wanted to be devoured by blood-thirsty demons. Arlene was the only one who slept. Some of the travelers stayed in the dinning hall drinking black Menellian tea and chatting. William and Wilson played a board game.

"You can't do that!" argued William. He tried to point to the mistake on the board with his bandaged arm that stretched around his neck.

"Yes I can, William. I can move my king anywhere on the board as long as I go backwards, forwards, and side-to-side."

"You move your queen! Not king!"

Beyond the land of Hermalie laid the Forbidden Island. In the Hell Castle, Raven sat in the middle of the dark room lit with black candles. Her eyes were closed and she chanted to herself. Xander paced himself back and forth and waited impatiently. Raven stopped and then looked up at her son.

"The princess has returned to Menellia." she said.

She lifted herself up and walked over to the cauldron. It was filled with a green liquid. She waved her hand over it and an image of Arlene appeared. She was fast asleep in her bed.

"She is the Seventh Angel?" asked Xander." She doesn't look like a threat."

Raven moved her bony index finger from side to side in front of his face.

"Wrong. The Menellian princess is more wise and powerful than the last chosen ones. Her name is Arlene Leggora. The daughter of Prince Daniel. Twenty two years ago I sent an army to kill the chosen one. But of course the demons failed."

"So what do I do?"

"You are going to finish her off. Tonight! As she is laying in bed. I'm sure you are a smart boy. Use your imagination."

Xander took over the place where his mother was standing. He closed his eyes and held himself still. When he opened them he found himself standing on red clouds. And there was Arlene's bed floating on the clouds and Arlene was fast asleep in it. He started to study her face.

"So this is the Seventh Angel."

Arlene opened her eyes and looked around before looking up at him.

"Where am I?" she asked.

"You're still dreaming, Arlene Leggora. You are still asleep, "he answered.

Arlene lifted herself off her bed and stood on the red

clouds.

"Who are you?" she asked. She wasn't sure if she should be afraid of this stranger.

"Oh, forgive me," Xander said sarcastically. "I am Xander Darkshadow. Son of Raven Darkshadow."

After hearing Raven's name Arlene knew that she was in trouble of some sort.

"She's the one who killed my mother and father, so we suspect."

"Hmmm….Twenty two years ago demons were sent to kill the Seventh Angel. They failed to do so. And now I have come to finish what my mother started."

A dagger appeared in his right hand. Arlene, realizing that she was completely defenseless, began to run for her life.

"Where are you going to run off to, Arlene. You're trapped inside your own dream."

He held out his free hand and Arlene was magically dragged backwards. He grabbed her arm and pointed the dagger at her heart.

"No! Please! Don't!" she cried.

"How pathetic," said Xander. "the Seventh Angel, the hero, is begging for her life. I almost felt sorry for you, Arlene Leggora."

Without another word the dagger plunged itself into Arlene's chest.

*   *   *

In the Menellian Castle, Arlene's screams echoed from her room down the castle halls. Eron, reading silently in his guest room, perked up his Elf ears.

"Arlene?"

As quickly as he could he sprinted through the halls, up staircases, and into Arlene's room. He opened the door and walked in. There he saw the silent and motionless Arlene.

She stared up at the ceiling and didn't even blink.

"Arlene, are you ok?" he asked.

But she didn't say or do anything. Her eyes were still focused on the ceiling.

He walked over to her side.

"Arlene?"

She still laid motionless. He felt her skin and she was cold. He put her hand on his chest and he didn't feel a heartbeat. When he removed his hand, his palm was covered in her blood. He shook her shoulder.

"Arlene!" he shouted.

She was lifeless. Eron ran out of the room and tried to look for help.

"ROZIN! GLORIA!" he shouted.

He ran into Evensen who was admiring statues and paintings in the hallways.

"Evensen!" cried Eron.

'Young Whitestone, what has happened?"

Eron was shaking and the trill in his voice made him stutter.

"It...it's Arlene. She...she's not bre...breathing! He...her heat! It...It's"

"Hold on there, I know where this is going to. Call for Arlene's family. I'll warn Rozin."

They both headed into opposite directions. Evensen galloped through gigantic hallways, down staircases, and into a room where Rozin chatted with Sama.

"Rozin! Sama!" cried Evensen.

"What is it, Evensen?" asked Sama.

"Miss Leggora. Young Eron said that she isn't breathing and something about her heart. I fear that her soul has been taken. I do not know how."

They ran out and headed to Arlene's room. Once they walked in they spotted Gloria holding Arlene's hand. Tears flowed from her brown eyes. Her chin was trembling.

"The child is gone," she said softly." the child has passed."

Eron walked in with Nick and Harmony. Along with Darwin and the twins. Darwin fell to his knees and cried in his hands. Both William and Wilson tried to hold back their tears.

William sat down by Arlene and rested his forehead on his free palm. Then ran his fingers through his blonde hair. Gloria hugged him and cried on his shoulder.

"Don't weep for Arlene, friends," Harmony said." miracles can happen. And anyone can make them. Raven can take a life but we can give it back."

Nick took her hand and they moved to the dead Arlene. William and Gloria moved out of the way for them. Nick went to one side of the bed and Harmony stood on the other.

They lifted their arms and chanted together :

"Life shall give and evil shall take,
Destroy the soul thee can make,
Zeles we call to thee from heaven,
Bring back our fallen. Restore the Seven.
Come forth, The Seventh Angel.
Come back to the Land of the Heavens."

Arlene's body lit up as a swirl of pink and blue flew into her body.

"Arise, Arlene Leggora," said Nick. "The Seventh Angel."

Arlene took a deep breath in and then her body was normal and the swirl disappeared. she sprung forward in her bed and looked up at everyone.

"Where is he!" she shouted. "He tried to kill me!"

She covered her ears and hid her face in her arms.

"I hate this! I hate my life! I hate that sword! Why am I still living!? Why can't I die!?!? I want to die!!"

Harmony reached for her arm.

"Don't touch me there!!!" she screamed. "He touched me there!!!"

"Who touched you, Arlene," asked Harmony. "what happened?"

Arlene was sweating and tears flowed from her eyes.

"He said that his name was Xander, "she admitted, "Xander Darkshadow, he wanted to kill me! He knew about the day I was born."

"Who is Xander Darkshadow?" asked Darwin.

"It can only mean one thing," Harmony turned her attention to Rozin." It seems that Raven has a son. If he is able to enter Arlene's dream, he is, no doubt, a dream leaper. She knows Arlene has returned to Menellia. She is trying to stop Arlene since the twins were born. Raven did know that Arlene was the chosen one."

Nick paused then held Arlene's hand. Eron hugged her tightly.

"I thought I lost you forever. I never want to lose you again."

*　　*　　*

It was now January thirteenth. Arlene and Nick had turned twenty three. In front of the castle, people were dancing to a small band. The singer was the same woman who sang on the streets. One Menellian man played on big drums and two others played on guitars. Eron danced with Arlene, Nick with Harmony, and Rozin with Gloria. Arlene was having the time of her life. Menellians were bowing to her and wished her a happy birthday. It was what Arlene had always wanted. A birthday that she had always wanted. After the party Arlene stood on the balcony and looked at the starry sky. Eron was beside her and he cleared his throat.

"Arlene, I have something for you."

He opened his hand and he handed her a silver ring.

"Happy birthday."

Arlene looked closer at the stone. It had a moon inside of it. Then a shooting star glided across the moon in the ring.

"Eron!" she cried. "It's beautiful."

She put it on her finger.

"I don't know how to thank you."

He took her by her hand gently.

"It's wonderful how Afelle has blessed me with you. What greater gift can come from the heavens?"

Arlene began to speak in Menellian.

"Mind telling me what you said?"

Arlene smiled.

"No matter where life will take me, I will always love you."

He took her into his arms and gave her a gentle kiss.

* * *

The next morning there was a knock at the castle door. Nick walked over and answered it.

"For the royal Menellian family," said the Menellian man. "message from the Bensen Palace.

Nick thanked him before accepting the letter and shutting the door. He took the ribbon off the blue envelope and read the message. Harmony entered the foyer.

"What is it, Nick?" she asked.

"We have an invitation, my lady. The king of the Bensen Palace has invited us to a celebration dinner."

He handed Harmony the letter and she began to read it:

"To the lady of the Menellians and to the Elf king of Lindolin City;

I, King Edward James Stewart Johnathan Andrew Richard Bensen, invite you to attend the celebration dinner party. The celebration is for my son, Prince Thomas Bradley Christopher Lance Franklin Philip Bensen, on his engagement to Princess Miranda Guenvil of the Guenvil Palace. We wish that you shall come and we willl prepare for your arrival.

I await for you,

King Edward James Stewart Johnathan Andrew Richard Bensen"

"You'd think that his hand would cramp up after writing their long names," joked Harmony.

"I wonder how he figured out about King Rozin staying here," said Nick. "will we attend?"

"Of course we are. I do not see why not. King Edward and I have been really good friends since we were children."

"How did that come to be?"

"It's a long story, child."

"I'm patient."

"Very well."

Harmony let out a sigh and began with her story.

"When my father was king he'd always visit the Bensen Palace because I think that he was really good friends with the king and queen. I remember wandering through their garden. I was only ten at that time and I was smelling the flowers that the Bensen Palace planted. I really liked them and I remember wishing that we had their types of flowers here in Menellia. In my opinion, red roses smell better than black roses.

"Then I felt something on the back of my head. I looked down and I saw that it was a pebble. A small silver pebble. I looked around and I didn't see anyone or anything. I continued to smell the flowers until I felt it again. It was another silver pebble.

"I looked again and I saw some blonde hair poking out of the bushes. I waved my little finger in the air and he flew into the sky. I can still remember the look that he gave. Poor child was frightened. Then I threw him into the nearest fountain."

Harmony began to laugh in pleasure at this memory.

" 'Nasty little human!' I said. 'Why are you throwing pebbles, boy!' He looked up at me and said, ' You're a trespasser! Get out or I am telling father!'

" 'I am the Princess of Menellia! I can go where I please!' I was really sassy with him in my childhood days. But that all changed over time."

"It sounds like you two didn't give each other a very well first impression," laughed Nick.

"True but the first impressions don't really determine the future. We didn't get along at first but then we started to become fast friends. Now if you think about it, my dear Nick, you gave Arlene a bad impression, as well."

*   *   *

In the afternoon Arlene and Eron walked around the public square.

"It is going to be so exciting!" cheered Arlene. "we have just been invited to the king's party! I always wanted to meet the royal Bensen family."

"I have," said Eron. "They are great rulers of the human race. Their army is strong, their villages are grand, and everything there is beautiful."

"I wish tomorrow were here all ready. It makes me so happy that I am no longer a slave."

From behind the happy couple they could hear the snickering of girls.

"Who'd of thought that the Princess of Menellia was......a slave."

It was Demetra and Topenga.

"So you're not so great as they say, right? I guess no one here in Menellia knows that the so called 'Seventh Angel' was nothing but a bloody backed floor scrubber."

"She was hand picked by the angels themselves," broke in Eron. "it's shame to see young ladies, like yourselves, not drop to your knees and bow down to your hero."

As you can see Elves are not the greatest in come backs, but at least Eron made a good point. Demetra gave the Elf a dirty look.

"You Elves think your so much smarter than any other race in Hermalie. You're so pathetic in the way you all talk. Such goody-goodies. Your people are even afraid of a little magic! Then again, I guess we all can't be as powerful as Menellians."

Arlene wanted to smack her, but Eron was doing nothing more but just "turning the other cheek" like all Elves do.

"If she is such a hero," Demetra continued. "then she wouldn't be afraid to face me in a broomstick race. I'm in the mood for competition."

"Fine!" said Arlene. "I accept."

"Meet us in the woods, and no turning back!"

Demetra and Topenga walked away.

"Why did you accept?" asked Eron. "The race is just a waste of time."

"You're right," said Arlene. "It's just that....what she said about me being a slave and the nasty words she said about you and your people. It made me lose my mind. And I am not good at riding a broomstick. But what can I do now? I can't turn back."

Arlene and Eron returned to the castle and Arlene made her way to the broom storage. She grabbed a broom and she was just about to head off into the woods to meet up with Demetra and Topenga.

"And where do you think you are going?"

Nick caught her before she even attempted to leave.

"Ummm...er..."Arlene stuttered.

Nick gave her a stern look.

"What are you going to do with that broomstick, Arlene!"

Arlene had to give in.

"Demetra challenge me to a broomstick race in the woods. I accepted."

"Arlene! What were you thinking? Broomstick races can be deadly. Especially in the woods. What if you crash? Also, what Demetra failed to mention to you, broomstick races are illegal!"

"I'm sorry, but she said something horrible to me and Eron. I mentioned about being a slave and she overheard. We were in the public square."

"So you said 'yes' when she challenged you to a race. Just because you mentioned about being a slave?"

"No! She called me a bloody backed floor scrubber and she insulted Eron's people! I wanted to get back at her so badly. I'll do anything to make her take back all her words!"

"But remember what Aunt Harmony said? Revenge is evil, and anyone that uses revenge becomes evil."

"I can't turn back now!"

Nick slapped his forehead and looked back at her.

"You're right. You can't turn back now. You got into this mess and you are going to clean it up. Not only that now you have me mixed into it."

He grabbed a broomstick.

"No, Nick. You are right. I did get myself into this and I need to pay the consequences. You don't have to come."

"I HAVE to come. You need a second racer."

*   *   *

The twins got to the woods and saw Demetra and Topenga.

"What is he doing here?" Topenga asked.

"This is the rule of the race, "said Nick. "Each competitor has to have a partner in the race. You know that."

Demetra rolled her eyes.

"Well here are my rules for this race. We have to circle the city four times and we have to stay in the woods. Here is the starting point."

She pointed to the ground that she was standing on.

"This is the beginning and it is the ending. Laps end here, as well. That is it. Everything else is a free-bee."

The four mounted their broomsticks and they hovered in the air. Arlene's palms were sweating and she was shaking a little as she was looking down. It seemed as if the ground was moving to her eyes.

"You're not scared of heights, are you princess?" snickered Topenga.

"No! Of course not!" lied Arlene.

Demetra counted down from five to one and they were off. Demetra was in front of Topenga and Topenga was in front of Arlene and Nick.

"We have to get closer!" shouted Nick to Arlene. "But try your best to stay away from their brooms. They will knock you off!"

Arlene agreed to what he said and together they flew in front of Topenga.

"No fair!" she shouted.

Topenga took out four bottles of potion from her robe

pocket and began to throw them at Arlene and Nick. The bottles missed them as they exploded on the trees. Nick took his own bottle out of his pocket and he threw it at Topenga. A cloud of black smoke blinded her view. And she started losing control of her broom. She swerved and then managed to get back on track. Arlene flew her broom up to Demetra and Demetra studied her every move with the corner of her eye. She pulled a branch off of one of the bending trees and once Arlene got close enough Demetra swung the branch at her and it cut Arlene on the face. Nick took out two bottles and he threw them to Arlene.

"Aim for the back!" he shouted.

Arlene caught them and did what she was told. Just as they finished the first lap, she threw a bottle on the back of Demetra's broom. It exploded and Demetra lost control. She gained the control back but the back of her broom was engulfed in black smoke. Topenga was still behind Nick. They finished the second lap and Topenga took another bottle and threw it at the back of his broom. A huge BOOM filled the air and Nick crashed into one of the trees.

"Down for the count!" cheered Topenga.

Arlene turned and threw the remaining bottle at Topenga. Topenga's broom split and she flew into the air. Topenga hit the ground on her back and she growled in anger. Demetra and Arlene got to the third lap. And Arlene, forgetting what Nick said to her, flew to Demetra and stayed at her side. Demetra thrust her side at Arlene and tried to knock her off. Then a cloud of purple smoke surrounded them both. Arlene and Demetra stopped in the air. They couldn't move their brooms at all. And on the ground stood Harmony.

"Well, well, well. What do we have here?" she said as she looked up at them.

~CHAPTER 7
THE UNEXPECTED
GUEST~

Arlene had never seen her aunt become so angry before. The four stood in front of her. Arlene and Nick were the only ones who had guilt faces. Demetra and Topenga didn't seem to care.

"I'd expect this from children but never in my years would I see twenty three year olds, mature adults, cause such a chaos behind the city!"

Harmony continued.

"Do you realize what you have done? The people on the streets were panicking! The thought of war was going through their heads as you four were using magic against each other! What do you have to say about this?"

Arlene and Nick muttered their sorry with their heads down. Demetra and Topenga didn't show any pity and they didn't say anything.

"And I suppose you young ladies don't have a care in

the world about anything but yourselves!" said Harmony to them.

"My queen," broke in Topenga. "As I should speak for us all, it was just a broomstick race and not a war from Malenda herself. I see no reason to pity."

"You are too bold, Miss Jade! For you show a huge lack of judgment!" scolded Harmony. "This world has been under chaos since the Angels have created it! How dare you stand here and say to me that your act of foolishness was not harmful to not only yourselves but to the panic of the people!"

"Surely, the Seventh Angel will save us. And we'll be free to do whatever we want!" said Demetra sarcastically.

"Silence!" yelled Harmony. "Demetra Onyx, your pride will be the death of you! Your family, for many years, have looked to the sin of pride and followed nothing else...."

"Do not lecture me about my family!" interrupted Demetra. "Ever since the Leggoras have taken over the city of Menellia all you ever think about is how everyone else isn't as perfect as yourself!"

"That is not true!" snapped Harmony.

"Oh yes it is, my lady!" snapped back Demetra. "I know all about you Leggoras. Mother and father told me how much you all want things to be perfect,peaceful, and blessed.

You whip the people every time they put one toe out of your line!"

"All lies!" hissed Harmony. "Since the Onyx family lost the competition for the crown, your family followed the evil ways of revenge and say disgusting things about our family! The High Priest saw the darkness in the Onyx blood and that is the reason why the Leggora family still stands where they are now!"

Demetra heard no more and walked out of the castle with Topenga following her. Harmony sat down on her throne and laid her head in her hand.

"Aunt Harmony," Arlene started to say. "Demetra's family was suppose to rule Menellia?"

"They weren't suppose to, child," she said. "They are one of the most powerful Menellian families in the city, but we rank the top. The High Priest found in them a love for black magic and voodoo. He saw in the Leggoras hope, truth, patients, and pure love. After your great, great, great grandfather died the city was not sure if the Leggoras should continue with being the rulers. But we were voted to stay and here we are now. Still the royal family of Menellia."

"Well I have enjoyed this really, "lied Nick and he slowly walked backwards." but I think that I shall take my leave now."

"Not so fast, Nicholas Samuel!"

Harmony pointed her finger at him and he froze in his place.

"There is still more to come. Your punishment!"

"What exactly is that?" asked Nick.

He tried to move but his legs couldn't do it.

"I want you to clean each and every statue in the Great Halls. Knowing from all this hard work you two will learn your lessons."

She waved her hand in the air and a black dress appeared in Arlene's and along with a black bandana. In Nick's arms were a set of overalls and a loose black shirt.

Harmony gave Nick the power to move again.

"Now I suggest you get changed into your work clothes and get started."

Nick and Arlene began to walk out the door.

"Oh yes. I forget something for you, also."

Two brown rags fell on top of their heads. Nick and Arlene took them off and continued to walk out the door.

* * *

Once they were changed Arlene met up with Nick in the first Great Hall.

"Don't worry about the rags," said Nick. "there is an easier way to do this."

Harmony walked through the hall saying:" That wont work,my dear. Better put some of your elbow-grease into it."

So Arlene and Nick had no choice but to use the rags. Nick was having a hard time because he kept complaining that his arms and hands hurt. Arlene wasn't complaining at all.

"I'm use to this," she said. "I've been doing this my whole life. Besides this is mercy compared to what Aunt Mary use to do to me if ever I did something wrong."

"What happened to you that was so cruel?" asked Nick as they moved to the next statue.

"Why her whip, of course," said Arlene. "In Alexandrite, if a slave did something wrong, they get ten whacks."

Arlene moved her sleeve from her shoulder and revealed her scars from the whip.

"Good Angels!" cried Nick. "There is no mercy for a

slave."

"Not at all." said Arlene.

They went back to cleaning the statue.

"This is my absolute favorite," he admitted.

Arlene looked at the statue. It was a statue of a woman with long wavy hair. It was flowing with her dress.

"Who is she?" asked Arlene.

Nick smiled and said: "It's our mother. And I must say she looks a lot like you."

Arlene looked up at the statue and gazed into it's eyes.

"Sometimes," began Nick. "if you look at her, and she is looking at you, it's almost as if you can hear her voice in the wind."

Arlene heard the wind outside blowing through the windows. With the wind, she thought that she could hear the singing of a woman.

"I think I can hear her, too," she said. "I think even though her body is gone, her soul lives here in Menellia. I think that she is everywhere. She lingers with us forever. No matter where we are."

*   *   *

Arlene and Nick finished cleaning all the statues. William and Wilson entered skipping down the hall like children.

"Arlene! Arlene!" William cried out. "forget about the past, princess."

He started twirling Arlene around and began to dance with her.

"Don't look upon us as slaves anymore. Don't even say the word. We are invited to the party of Prince

Thomas for he is engaged to the beautiful Princess Miranda. Well she is not as beautiful as you of course."

William stopped and looked at Arlene's outfit. And then looked at Nick next.

"I must say that isn't the way the royal family should look."

"We were punished, William," said Arlene.

"I see," said Wilson." I guess my brother and I shall take our leave. We must choose our own outfits for tomorrow's occasion. Ta! Ta!"

William and Wilson each grabbed one of Arlene's hands and kissed them.

*　　*　　*

The next day Arlene spent most of the time getting ready for the dinner party. Arlene's maids helped her with her dress, hair, and her make-up.

"Can I ask why black is mainly worn here?" asked Arlene.

"Black is a part of Menellian culture, my lady," said one of the maids. "black is our protection color."

Arlene didn't understand.

After getting ready Arlene walked to the unicorn stable where Nikita waited impatiently. Nikita was all set and prepared to take Arlene to the Bensen Palace.

"Ready for our next destination, Nikita?"

Arlene stroked her long mane and guided her out of the stables. Arlene and Nikita made it to the front of the city. And Arlene was surprised to see the Onyx and the Jade family with the group. All Menellians had black unicorns while the Elves, Arlene, and Darwin and the twins had white.

"How insulting," said Topenga. "the Menellian princess is riding on the back of an Elf's unicorn."

Arlene ignored her.

Nick, to Arlene, looked really handsome in his formal wear.

His black unicorn stuck close to him as he walked up to her.

"Arlene, I want you to meet a really good friend of mine."

He pulled his unicorn a little further to him.

"This is Liberty."

Arlene wanted to reach down and pat Liberty on the head but Nikita knocked Arlene's hand out of the way with her head.

"Stubborn for an Elvish unicorn," laughed Nick.

Nikita looked at him as if she knew what he was talking about.

"This is Nikita." introduced Arlene. "she was a gift to me from the Whitestone family."

Liberty walked forward but Nikita whinnied furiously and caused the black unicorn to move back.

"He gets intimidated easily," said Nick.

He got onto Liberty and Arlene tapped Nikita on the head.

"Mind your manners!" she scolded.

Rozin and Harmony led the way to the Bensen Palace. They were followed by invited Menellians and the party from Lindolin City. Arlene got a glimpse of Demetra's family. The mother and father seemed so mysterious. Both wearing long, black, flowing cloaks and serious faces. Demetra's mother was absolutely beautiful but

Arlene thought she'd look so much better if she smiled. Demetra's father gave her a chill down her spine. He didn't seem like the type to talk to. Riding along side Demetra, on her graceful unicorn, was another girl. Unlike the rest of her family she wore her cloak hood down. She had dark hair like Demetra's and she looked younger. Arlene knew it had to be Demetra's younger sister. The journey from Menellia to the Bensen Palace didn't seem as long as the last journey Arlene took. The Bensen Palace was white as snow. A shimmer of crystal beamed on the faces of the guests as the winter sun shined down on the castle.

"The Bensen Palace never changes," Arlene heard Harmony say. "it's as beautiful as Heaven."

The pearl gates opened and the guests were greeted by smiling faces.

"William, Darwin, we've just stepped into Utopia!" said Wilson with a smile on his face.

Stepping into the palace and watching the celebration made Arlene jump back in time. She remembered when Aunt Mary and Uncle Anthony threw parties and she wanted so much to be a part of it. Now she is. She stood alone, nervously, and watched the people dance. Darwin tried to follow the dancers as best as he could and William and Wilson looked at the paintings on the walls.

"I feel as if the artist is trying to say 'Never judge a book by it's cover' "said William.

The painting was awkward. Arlene couldn't even tell what the artist was trying to say. She didn't even like it. The royal Elf family bowed to the Bensen family and Princess Miranda of the Guenvil Palace.

"My lady!" shouted William and Wilson as they ran

up to Princess Miranda. "I should say you are looking marvelous, your highness." they said together.

They each grabbed one of her hands and began to kiss them. Princess Miranda frowned and jerked her hands away from them.

*   *   *

Sama sat by himself. His eyes were closed and he started humming a tune.

"Sama?" called Arlene. "Why are you here all alone?"

Sama looked up.

"Oh, I do not care for these types of events anymore," he said sadly.

Arlene sat beside him.

"Is it because of the night my aunt and uncle died?"

"Aye, Arlene. It is."

"But, Sama, it shouldn't keep you from being happy."

Sama sighed.

"Nothing will make me happy, princess. Alexandrite was my home. My home was taken from me. I was born there and I hoped to die there. It's nothing but a lost hope to me now."

Sama was silent and he looked around.

"There are many dangers that lurk, Arlene."

He pulled the Sword of the Seventh Angel out of his cloak.

"Keep this wherever you go. Never let it leave your sight. It is your life, now. Use it with care."

He handed it to Arlene.

"Sama, you make it sound like you are going to die."

"No, Arlene. Not today. Not tomorrow. You have

your destiny. And I think it's about time that you pay extra attention to whatever is going on."

"I don't understand."

Arlene thought about it.

"Is something coming?"

Eron walked up to her and held out his hand to her.

"May I have this dance?"

Arlene still had her eyes fixed on Sama. Sama didn't make eyes contact and didn't answer her question. Arlene then took Eron's hand and they walked to the middle of the room.

"What happened?" he asked as they began to dance.

"Something that I don't understand."

*   *   *

Nick stood alone and stared at the dancers. Demetra walked up to him and stood by his side. Nick tried to ignore her by turning his face.

"All alone?" she said.

Nick stayed silent.

"How rude and I was just trying to make nice..."

"You're looking for trouble!" Nick interrupted.

Demetra gave a sour look. They were silent again.

"Where is Piper?" he asked.

"I would hope you'd dance with me," said Demetra.

"Where-is-your-sister?" demanded Nick.

Demetra threw her head to the direction where Piper was standing. Nick walked away from her.

"Men," she muttered under her breath.

Nick cleared his throat and walked up to Piper.

"Piper Onyx?"

"Your majesty?" she said bowing.

"Would you care to dance, my lady?"

Piper nervously tucked some of her dark hair behind her white pointy ear and said: "Yes, you're majesty."

Nick and Piper joined the other dancers.

"I must say, Piper, you look amazingly young for a woman of nineteen."

"Your majesty, I am only seventeen."

"Oh...pardon..."

*   *   *

Rozin, Harmony, and Gloria spent their time talking with the royal family of Bensen.

"My son is finally getting married!" King Edward said proudly. "Thomas has always been my favorite son. It's been my dream for him to become a king. A great one at that."

"Oh, Father," said Thomas. "You know I learn from the best. But um....my brother, Francis......I always thought that he was for favorite."

"That boy couldn't tell a lance from a sword," said King Edward.

Gloria took a bow for Princess Miranda. Miranda just stood there and didn't even look at her.

"Blessings onto you, dear princess. May Afelle grant you much love."

Miranda sneered.

"As sweet as you are, Princess Glorifia, I do not care for the prayers of Elves."

Gloria rose and glared at Miranda.

"Well then? Care not for the blessing. Then damn you

to Malenda."

Miranda's eyes widened.

"How dare you say such a hateful thing to me!"

"On the contrary, princess, it is a sin to be a hypocrite."

"That is enough, Glorifia!" yelled Rozin.

Gloria walked away and Rozin followed.

"How could you?" snapped Gloria. "letting that bitter princess say that about us!"

"Most royal humans do not care about Elves! It is the way they are!" explained Rozin. "And as Elves, we do not say curse words! Let her be and cleanse yourself from your sin! We do not hope for ANY human to be the demon of Malenda."

Gloria nodded and comprehended.

*   *   *

All guests were seated and they held up their goblets of wine. The king, prince, and princess stood in front of everyone hand-in-hand. The king had his goblet raised.

"To the future king and queen of the Bensen Palace. May the blessings and good karma rain upon you both this very night. And guide you to be great rulers of Bensen's future. And forever may you be the heart and soul of Hermalie."

"Long live the king and queen!" everyone said. Except for Gloria. Everyone drank to the kings wishes, but Gloria threw the wine over her shoulder. Then the room started to shake. The candles flickered and the wine in the goblets began to move from the vibration. Glasses fell off tables and the rumbling was louder. Menelliansm, Elves, and humans began to panic.

"The world is restless!" said Darwin.

But Darwin was wrong. Black clouds began to form inside the castle. The gigantic double doors that led into the Great Hall flew open and Xander Darkshadow appeared.

"Sorry that I am spoiling all the fun."

The crowd looked at him in fear.

"Xander Darkshadow," whispered Arlene.

"Who?" questioned Eron.

"He is the son of Raven the witch."

Xander looked around the room and then at the royal humans.

"Them? The heart and soul of Hermalie? I couldn't help but laugh at that sentence," chuckled Xander.

"I demand you leave at once!" shouted King Edward.

Xander lifted his hand at the king. The king was gasping for air and he held onto his neck. He was lifted into the air as Xander raised his arm.

"Let this be a reminder to all who witness this night," began Xander. "as her loyal servant, as well as my mother, Hermalie will belong to Raven Darkshadow and her Angel, Malenda, Lady of Hell. Humans, Menellians, and Elves will perish. There is only one that can stop us. The REAL heart and soul of Hermalie."

The king's eyes were cloudy. There was a loud snap and the king laid his head to the side. He was dropped and he fell dead to the ground.

"No!" shouted the prince.

"Edward!" shrieked Harmony.

"There is only one," began Xander again. "The Seventh Angel. The heroine of Hermalie. The chosen one of the Heavenly Angels. But sadly, like your king, she died by the hands of a Darkshadow."

"I think not!"

Arlene stood behind him with the tip of the Sword of the Seventh Angel pointing at him.

"Impossible," he said.

"You can't break the heart of a Leggora."

"I did it once, Princess. I can do it again. Your not as strong as you think you are. If the death of your mother and father doesn't prove how fragile a Leggora can be then I guess the second death of Arlene Leggora will prove otherwise."

He took off his cloak and drew his sword.

"Let's play again, shall we?"

"I'm up for a sword play, Xander."

Arlene's improvement with a sword increased. She was afraid of Xander but she swore never to show it. People stood in fear and yet excitement as Arlene and Xander fought. Nick was ready to step in if ever Arlene needed him to.

"I see your thoughts and I know your fears," said Xander. "You're afraid to fail. Afraid to let the Angels and Hermalie fall."

Arlene tried not to listen to him. She continued to fight and he continued to scare her.

"Your aunt and your twin will suffer the same fate as your parents!"

Arlene was angry.

"Your friends will disappear and you will be the same as before. Nothing but a servant girl! A no one! The old Arlene Leggora!"

"No!" she shouted.

Her mind was being distracted by her failures and the

loss of everyone that she loves. Xander struck her left shoulder. Arlene screamed in pain and she fell.

"Pathetic. That is all you'll ever be. Your as weak as the last two. I can all ready feel Hermalie in my hands."

He took the blade out of her left shoulder and struck her right. She screamed and cried in pain. Nikita burst through the doors and charged after Xander. She began to trample him and scare him. Nick ran to the rescue and struck Xander in the back with his sword. Xander pulled it out and ran into the darkness.

The people of the Bensen Kingdom mourned the death of their king. Prince Thomas, angered, swore his revenge.

"Revenge leads to Malenda, Thomas." said Harmony.

"This is your fault!" yelled Thomas." All of you. Especially her!"

He pointed at Arlene.

"Because of all of you, my father lies dead and there is war on my kingdom! From this moment on no Menellian, Elf, or HER and her friends shall be able to step into the Bensen Kingdom. If that new law is disobeyed you will be considered a threat and executed!!!!"

Prince Thomas turned to the crowd.

"All Menellians leave now! Never return! You can thank your rulers for that!!!"

Harmony fell into anger.

"You cannot blame the Elves, Menellians, nor my niece for the death of Edward!! War is on all of us!! And it has been that way for thousands of years!! Hermalie is our world and it is up to all of us to fight for it!! I know that is what your father would want!!!"

"You have no right to tell me what to do! I am king

now! And I say I am not going to turn into a burden for your niece's so called 'destiny'!!"

"Your father was wrong," stepped in Arlene. "You're not the king he expected."

"LEAVE NOW!! OR I'LL HAVE YOU ALL HANGED TONIGHT!!!"

They didn't say another word and everyone began to walk out of the palace.

"Excellent job, Princess Arlene, "Topenga said in her usual sarcasm.

"Because of you we are all doomed to Hell, "said Demetra.

At that point Arlene began to hate herself.

*   *   *

When they arrived back at Menellia Darwin and Eron began patching up Arlene's wounds. Arlene cried silently.

"Arlene?" questioned Darwin.

Arlene turned her face.

"I hate my life. I hate myself."

"Arlene, do not say such a thing," said Eron.

"Why!" she yelled. "The king is dead! The king is dead because of me!!"

"Arlene, do not let Thomas feed you that," said Eron. "You did what you had to do. One human is dead but imagine how many more there would be if you didn't fight? And you were brave. You will make a difference. You are the…"

"Seventh Angel!! I know!! Nothing but everyone is counting on!! You all don't get it!! But I am feeling like a servant again!!"

She grabbed the bottle of healing potion, threw it up against the wall, and stormed out of the room.

*   *   *

Arlene sat on her bed and stared at the sword. She stared at it for hours.

"What if I do fail?" she said to herself. "Am I suppose to live this way? Miserable? Never! I'll end my own suffering."

She walked slowly to the sword and picked it up. She walked to the middle of the room and looked up at the painting of Kirlana.

"You disappoint me," she said to the painting. "people look to you and you deprive them of the one thing they need most. Happiness. You can easily stop Malenda than a warrior Elf, my aunt, or a slave like myself. Yet you expect ME to save these people? I no longer want to be the Seventh Angel."

Arlene held up the sword and pointed the blade at her body. She stood there shaking. She looked at the ring that Eron gave her and saw the star shoot across the moon. She closed her eyes and tears ran down her face. She dropped the sword and sobbed in her hands.

"If I don't have the bravery of taking my own life, then how can I save this world?"

~CHAPTER 8
MERMAID BEACH
AND THE
DRAGON'S DWELLING~

"Arlene!" called out Darwin." Arlene, wake up!"
"I'm awake."
"In that case, can I come in? I have breakfast for you."
"I'm not hungry."
"But I have here eggs, fresh baked bread, fruit and some of Gloria's famous herb tea that you love so much."
"No, thank you."
Darwin sat the tray down and opened the door. Arlene sat on her bed and twirled the sword on the floor with her fingertips. The end of the blade started making a hole in the floor.
"Arlene, you look so sick. Did you sleep at all?"
Arlene shook her head.

"Are you still angry from yesterday?"

She didn't answer.

"Do you wish to sleep now?"

She didn't answer.

"Arlene, please talk to me."

She still sat in silence.

"I understand."

Darwin quietly walked out of the room.

"I wish I wasn't the Seventh Angel, Darwin," said Arlene.

Darwin paused and looked behind him again.

"I know. I know that you are having a hard time coping with all this. I am, too. This is a big change for us. You, me, William and Wilson. A very big leap. We're slaves one day and now here we are. All of us helping you save the world. To tell you the truth, Arlene. I'm scared, also. But the thing is we have to concur our fears together. There are so many things that everyone has to face. Because if we don't then we fail ourselves. So I ask you, my dear friend, will you face fear with me?"

Arlene always knew he had a way with words. Through thick and thin Darwin was always there for her. How could she deny what he just said?

"I'm always there, Darwin. I promise."

Darwin smiled.

"Wonderful. Now wait here."

Darwin walked out of the room. He returned minutes later with a goblet in his hand.

"Drink this."

He handed the goblet to her. Arlene raised the goblet to her lips and began to drink. After finishing it she felt dizzy and her eyelids were heavy. She dropped the goblet and fell onto her pillow.

"Sorry, Arlene," said Darwin as he picked up the goblet. "but you need to sleep."

*   *   *

Hours later Arlene woke up after the potion wore off. She felt alive again. And she felt refreshed.

"I'll thank Darwin later."

Meanwhile, Sama sent a message to Rozin from the village of Bensen.

"Lord Rozin Whitestone;

I am staying here in Bensen to catch up on myself. I have fallen under gloom after last night. But I know of whom that can help Arlene with her quest. My dragon, Merdoc. He is my loyal friend and you can trust him whole-heartedly. Give him my pendent as proof that you are allies. I hope for Kirlana's blessings onto you. I wish you all luck.

Sama Harless"

Rozin held the pendent in his hand. He slipped it over his head and let it dangle from his neck.

"And where do we go from here?" asked Harmony.

"We cannot stay in Menellia anymore, Harmony. Arlene has a job to do and we are her supporters. Now that the king of Bensen Palace is dead the prince will want nothing to do with the rest of us. The humans will want to set aside from this affair. I will round up our party. We are heading to the Hills of the Dragons. Sama says here that he has a friend who is, unfortunately, a dragon."

Harmony lifted an eyebrow.

"A dragon? How did Sama befriend a dragon?"

"I do not know," said Rozin. "but if it is what Sama recommends I will follow. Sama is wise. As for you, Queen Harmony, round up your best Menellian warriors. We will fight for freedom at the Forbidden Island."

"Forbidden Island!" said Harmony in shock. "No one has ever attempted to step on the ground of the Forbidden Island."

"Then it is about time that we do."

*   *   *

"Arlene! Arlene!" shouted William.

Arlene ran down the hall."

"What is it, William," she asked.

"Arlene! Word from Rozin. We are heading to the Hill of the Dragons. Sama's orders. I suggest you pack for another journey."

William turned and walked away. Then he stopped and turned back at Arlene. Arlene just stood there.

"You are ready for another journey, are you?"

Arlene looked down and thought about what Darwin said. She looked back up. This time with a smile.

"I am ready for another journey."

"Excellent!" said William and he headed off.

Arlene packed all her belongings and changed into another gown. The last thing that she grabbed was the sword. She gripped the handle and took a good look at it before putting it into the sheath. Before walking out of her room she took a look around. She remembered the music playing outside her bedroom window and her dance with Eron. She shut the door slowly.

"Arlene?" she heard someone say behind her.

She turned and saw Evensen.

"Hello, Evensen."

"Heading to Harmony?" he asked.

Arlene nodded. Evensen patted his back.

"Hop on. Trust me. It will be quicker."

"Really?" said Arlene.

She had never rode the back of a Centaur. Arlene hopped onto Evensen's back.

"Hold on!" he said.

Arlene gripped his white horse hair. Evensen sped off down the hallways and staircases. Until he reached the Great Hall. Arlene jumped off Evensen's back.

"Thanks, Evensen. That was fun."

Evensen bowed his head.

Arlene turned from Evensen and saw Harmony.

"Aunt Harmony, I want to thank you for everything that you have done. Thank you for showing me home and I hope to return soon."

Harmony, with tears in her eyes, ran over and hugged her.

"Oh, child," she said whipping her eyes. "You be careful out there. Keep the faith in yourself."

* * *

Arlene walked outside and the rest of them waited patiently for her. Eron handed Nikita over to her. Arlene looked around.

"Where is Gloria?"

"She went back to Lindolin City," said Eron. "she is

rounding up an army of Elves. For now we have to head off to the Dragon's Keep."

Arlene looked at the party. There was Darwin, William, Wilson, Eron, Rozin, Evensen, and herself.

"Is this all?" she asked.

"No," she heard someone say behind her.

"I want to come along," said Nick.

"But, Nicholas," said Harmony.

"I want to help my sister, Aunt Harmony. I promise. It is not for revenge."

Nick took Harmony by the hand and kissed it. Harmony kissed him on the forehead.

"I love you," she said.

*　　*　　*

The completed party began to move out of Menellia.

"Prince Nick!"

"Piper?"

Piper ran after Nick and she held something in her hand.

"Prince Nick, I wish to give you something. For luck."

She handed him a stunning gold pendent.

"Thank you, Piper."

Piper smiled. She wrapped her arms around Nick's neck. She brought him down to her height so she could kiss him. Then she took off. Nick fingered the pendent and smiled as she ran off to the city.

The Hills of the Dragons were on the other side of the land of Hermalie. It would take days to get there. But, before anyone could enter the hills, they need to know the password.

"The only way to figure out the password is through the mermaids," said Rozin to Arlene.

"We're going to see the mermaids?" asked Arlene with excitement.

"Do not get too excited, "said Evensen. "for mermaids are not friendly. They care for themselves and are known to insult outsiders. It's going to be hard to get a clue from them."

As darkness began to cover Hermalie Field they were protected over night in hollow trees from demons. The unicorns hid themselves, as well.

"Smart creatures, unicorns are," said Eron. "horses would be panicking by now."

In the afternoon of the next day the party reached Mermaid Beach. Mermaid Beach was like a tropical paradise. There was no snow covering the ground. It was really warm on the February month. The air was clean and the sand was a bright as the sun. The ocean was as blue as the cloudless sky.

"It's so beautiful here," said Arlene in awe.

"Mermaids are magical beings. They create their own Utopia. They hate sharing it," said Evensen.

The party walked onto the beach and that is when the mermaids started poking their heads out of the water.

One started saying:

"Intruders! Intruders! Eight intruding intruders!"

Another said:

"How dare they intrude on our land! We should bury them in the sand!"

And another said:

"I say drown them in the ocean today! A nice and slow death to make them pay!"

Arlene thought they were beautiful. All of them had long hair decorated with flowers. Their fins looked as if they were covered in diamonds. For gorgeous creatures they had ugly attitudes.

"Excuse our intrusion," said Rozin. "but we are here on a mission."

One said:

"A mission! Such suspicion! Maybe they are here for some fishin' "

Another said:

"We'll take them apart limb by limb! Walking on our land is a sin!"

"We're not here to kill mermaids," interrupted Arlene. "we need to get to the Hills of the Dragons."

The mermaids started chanting:

"The Hills of the Dragons are not for you! You failed your mission! What will you do? What will you do?"

The mermaids started laughing.

"If you do not give us the clue," started Evensen, "Raven and the Angel of Hell, Malenda, will destroy Hermalie. And everything you see before you will be dark, dead, black, and mermaids.........will be a myth."

The Mermaids gasped:

"The dirty Centaur threatened us. But let's not make a fuss. Stupid Centaur, can't you see? Angel of Hell is our queen."

"Aye,but let's take our chances, I didn't like his tone. We'll give them the clue. Then they will leave us alone."

"Don't be foolish, little one. First we gotta have some fun. We shouldn't give up so easily. So leave the little girlie to me."

Arlene was dragged down the sand magically and then she was in the water. One of the mermaids grabbed her by her long brown hair and held a dagger at her neck.

"Never ever will you enter the hill! Leave our land or it is her blood that will spill."

Arlene grabbed her sword from the sheath and held it over the water. The mermaids screamed the most ear-shattering screams Arlene has ever heard. They swam away and cuddled together by a rock.

One said:

"The Seventh Angel! The Seventh Angel!"

Another said:

"An evil, freakish, little devil!"

The last one said:

"We swear to Malenda we'll give you the clue!"

Then they all said:

"Angel number seven, we surrender to you!"

Arlene swam back to the shore.

"Good!" she said as she lifted herself to her feet. "Now give us the clue or suffer the consequences!"

She raised the sword and pointed it to the mermaids. The mermaids began to shake and two of them were crying. One of them slowly swam forward and gave out the clue:

"Beyond the hills
the dragons dwell;
In the
keeps lies fire in a well;
Beyond the
thorns of the cave's dripping blood;
There lies the lord and you are his beloved.
The way you taste and the way you scream;
Is like the fright in your dream.
Once you see him you will never be the same.
Can you figure out his name?"

Arlene turned to the others for help. Wilson started repeating the rhyme to himself.

"A lord?" questioned Wilson.

"Lord of the Dragons," said William.

"A wizard perhaps?" said Darwin.

"I don't think so," said Eron. "she mentioned that he likes our taste. The lord is a dragon."

Arlene raised the sword again to the mermaids. The mermaids shivered.

"More clues!" Arlene demanded.

The mermaids said:

"What's done is done! You only receive one!"

Arlene drew it closer.

"I said another one!!"

The mermaids nodded their heads. The second mermaid gave the clue:

"His name lies within the stars. A name that is different from all of ours."

"The stars?" questioned Nick.

Nick began to think.

"According to Menellian Astronomy the colony of stars that form a dragon is called Draco."

"The colony of Draco you are correct. But the name you are not to figure out yet."

"Draco is not the name of the dragon?" said Nick curiously.

Arlene held up the sword again.

"I demand one more!"

The third and final mermaid moved forward:

"The Menellians call a dragon by this name. You can figure this out! It isn't a game!"

"The Menellian word for 'dragon' is 'sen'. 'Sen' means

'evil creature' meaning a dragon or demon."

"So what does it have to do with the stars?" asked Rozin.

Arlene began to think.

"Draco and Sen have to by mixed together. Dracosen? Sendraco?…Dracsen?…"

"Dracsen! Dracsen!" the mermaids cheered.

"Dracsen! Dracsen! It's his name! Pass the hills! You win today!"

"Today?" said William. "Name and today do not rhyme."

The mermaids stuck out their tongues at him and swam away.

"I've always hated mermaids," said Evensen. "there isn't a perfect creature in this world. No matter how beautiful."

*　　*　　*

The party continued back into the cold Hermalie Field. Arlene missed the warmth of the beach once they left. It took half a day to arrive at the hills. There was a door that stood in the middle of a mountain. It was a stone door with carving of dragons. It gave them all chills down their spines.

"Arlene?" said Rozin.

He gestured his head to the door. Arlene walked forward.

"Dracsen!" she shouted.

The earth began to shake. Small rocks started to fall from the mountain. Then the door began to slowly open. Once it did the earth settled and the remaining rocks fell to the ground.

"Well shall we?" said William. "Come along Daggar."

William and Daggar were the first to walk in. Followed by Darwin, Eron, Rozin, Evensen, Nick, and Arlene.

"Come on, Wilson," said Nick.

Wilson sighed and walked with the others. But then the doors began to close.

"Hurry, Wilson!" shouted Darwin.

Wilson ran forward and squeezed through the doors before the door shut completely.

"Oh no!" cried Wilson. "Henry was left behind!"

"He'll be ok," said Eron. "Trust me."

The party walked through the dead cave. The running lava gave them light.

"In the keep lies fire in a well," said Evensen repeating the first clue.

"This is nothing more than a dead man's tomb," said Nick.

The cave was decorated with skeletons. Skeletons of humans, Elves, horses and other farm animals.

"No wonder the cows are disappearing in Lindolin," said Eron.

William pulled off one of the arms off a skeleton and snuck up behind Arlene.

"Got ya!" he yelled as he laid the hand on Arlene's shoulder.

Arlene's scream echoed off the cave walls.

"It's ok, Arlene," laughed William. "It's just a hand."

Rozin grabbed the dead arm from William and threw it into the lava.

"Grow up, Sir Galind," he said strictly.

"Yes, sir, o' sour one!" laughed William again.

Rozin rolled his eyes. They continued to walk around the cave Wilson went on with pointless talking.

"I was just thinking about this," said Wilson. "What would we be if we were fruit? Saying that Rozin there is sour he'd maybe be a lemon. And if Arlene were a fruit she'd be a strawberry because she is sweet. And if I were a...."

"Wilson!" yelled the others.

"Sorry, sorry," said Wilson raising his hands in front of them. "I just have the creeps, that's all. I just tried to make a friendly conversation."

"I hate dragons," said Darwin. "They're evil beings. Their tall, with sharp claws, they breath fire, and..."he gulped."...they kill. They are the true pets of Malenda."

A small rock fell on top of Darwin's head. Darwin looked up but he didn't see anything.

"They're scaly and ugly...."he said as he continued to walk.

Then another rock fell onto his head. Darwin looked up and yet again he didn't see anything.

"I smell trouble," said Evensen as he sniffed the air.

He held up his staff while the other members of the party held up their weapons.

"I AM THE ALMIGHT DRACSEN!" said a booming voice. "SURRENDER NOW AND I WILL EAT YOU QUICKLY!"

"We fight to the death!" shouted Rozin with his sword ready.

A large head poked out from the darkness. The head of a dragon. He was a dark green colored dragon with yellow eyes. He stared at the party with serious eyes.

"UUGGHH!!" he moaned. "I don't have the guts to do

this. I'm not Dracsen."

The party lowered their weapons.

"And what possessed you to make us think that you were Dracsen?" asked Darwin.

"Why not?" said the dragon. "If you were bored you'd want to do something fun, too."

"So you're not going to eat us?" asked Wilson.

"Heck no!" said the dragon. "I don't eat humans. You're nothing but skin and bone. And don't get me started on Elves and Menellians. With those pointy ears, it's like eating nails. I like cows. Like them nice and plump. But lately I have been eating Dracsen's leftovers."

The dragon began to walk away.

"But, since you all are here, I could make an acceptance."

The dragon quickly turned his head and snapped his teeth at them. They all jumped in fear. The dragon pounded his large fist on the ground as he was laughing. He was causing the whole cave to shake.

"HA! HA! You all should have seen the looks on your faces!"

The dragon calmed he laughter and whipped a tear away from his eyes.

"Oh, I kill myself."

"Look we don't have time for this!" said Nick. "We are looking for a dragon. His name is Merdoc."

"That would be me," said the dragon. "So you've heard of me? I have been know to be the most fearful dragon in Hermalie. You all probably want fifteen minutes of fame. I don't blame you. I am a stud."

"We were sent to find you by Sama Harmless."

Merdoc looked at Rozin.

"Sama Harless? My Sama Harless?'

The group nodded.

"Sama Harless? Sama Harless. Tall guy, white beard. stupid clothes, Sama Harless?"

They shrugged and then nodded again. Rozin took the pendent off his neck and gave it to Merdoc. Merdoc took the pendent by one of his large claws and studied the pendent.

"Sammy!" he cried. "Sammy, I thought you forgot all about me."

"Hermalie is at war," said Rozin. "It would be wonderful if you joined our side in the battle."

Merdoc wrapped the pendent around his finger.

"I can't fight a war," he said sadly. "Sure back then I use to be the best. But I've been stuck her under Dracsen's power. I can't fly nor breath fire."

He sat down and he made the cave shake again.

"Whoever heard of a dragon that couldn't fly or breath fire." said Arlene trying to keep her balance in the restless cave.

"I'll prove it to you!"

Merdoc took in a lot of air. His cheeks were puffed up, he put his lips together, and let out a POOF! But all that came out was black smoke.

"What was Sama thinking?" said Darwin. "We came for a strong dragon. And all we get is an over-grown gecko with scales and wings, that he doesn't even know how to use."

Merdoc growled at Darwin.

"I thought you said you didn't like dragons!"

"I don't. But at least there would be one who was willing to fight on our side. But no! We get a coward!"

Merdoc growled harder and Darwin flinched a little.

"Look at you! You are afraid of me! Who's the coward now, you little shrimp!"

"That's enough!" scolded Rozin. "Whether you like it or not, Darwin, we are fighting in this war together. That is if Merdoc agrees to join us. I will make a deal with you, Merdoc. If you join us in this war, I will reunite you with Sama and teach you how to breath fire and fly."

"Little Elf man," said Merdoc. "You cannot do any of that stuff, also. How can you teach me?"

"I have been studying about the dragons for three hundred years, Merdoc. So what do you say?"

Merdoc stroked his dragon chin as he was thinking about Rozin's deal.

"Elf man, you got yourself a dragon."

A loud booming noise filled the cave.

"AH!" shrieked Merdoc. "It's Dracsen! Let's get out of here!"

The group headed to the entrance of the cave. Wilson rushed forward and tried to escape first. But, when he reached his escape, he bounced backwards and fell onto Nick.

Evensen pounded on the invisible wall but it blocked the way to freedom.

"What is going on?" he asked.

"It's Dracsen!" said Merdoc. "Dracsen is very powerful. Gifted with magic by the Angel of Hell. The only way to escape is through him. The price? Winner stands and loser falls."

"We have to fight Dracsen?" questioned Wilson.

"Duh!" said Merdoc.

The cave began to shake every time Dracsen got

closer.

"Good luck," said Merdoc as he tried to walk away.

"Hold it!" shouted Arlene. "You're staying."

"Aww, why?" complained Merdoc.

"Because a team sticks together!"

"You know what? You are right! I can do this! There is no way I am gonna let Dracsen push me around."

Dracsen appeared out of the darkness. He was a fierce looking dragon and he was much taller then Merdoc.

"Ya wanna piece of me?" said Merdoc holding up his dragon fists. "I'll give you the whole cake and candles! C'mon! Give me your best shot!"

Dracsen knocked Merdoc against the cave walls with his gigantic hand. Merdoc fell to the ground.

"Like...I said," he said as he was looking dazed. "You're on your own."

And his head dropped.

"Such a dragon," said Darwin sarcastically.

The unicorns outside tried to make it into the cave so they could help their masters but they were also blocked.

"Prepare for battle!" demanded Rozin.

The party drew their swords and were ready to fight. Dracsen was a strong dragon and it had to take more than eight to bring him down. The group dodged, ran, attacked but they were getting no where. Dracsen's fire lit up the cave and it was getting too hot for the party to bear. They all hid behind a boulder. Dracsen's fire lit up the cave once again. It was becoming more and more harder for them to breath.

'What do we do?" cried Darwin.

"We have to figure out a way to make the fire shoot his way!" said Nick.

"And how do we accomplish that?" asked Eron coughing.

Dracsen stomped his foot and an avalanche of rocks fell from the ceiling of the cave. They huddled together and tried to protect themselves. But Arlene guarded herself with her sword. The rocks bounced off the blade and then shot back up to the ceiling of the cave.

"Arlene!" shouted Eron. "Your sword! The Sword of the Seventh Angel is also a shield, remember? Use it to send the fire Dracsen's way! Trust me!"

Arlene nodded and worked up her bravery to walk out into the open.

"Hey! Dracsen! Over here!"

Dracsen looked at her and started swinging his claws at her. Dodging them scared her to death, but she thought of the fire that was about to be blown. Dracsen took in some black smoke that filled the cave.

'This is it,' she thought.

He blew out a fireball from his lips. Arlene held the sword in front of her. The fireball bounced off the blade and hurtled back to Dracsen. Dracsen roared in pain. He then tripped and fell into the well of lava. He was gone. Dracsen's curse lifted and the smoke was replaced with fresh air. The party cheered for Arlene and the unicorns waited happily for their masters. Merdoc woke up from unconsciousness.

"What'd I miss?"

~CHAPTER 9
THE GYPSY TOWN~

They escaped from the Hills of the Dragons and vowed never to return. Rozin whistled a beautiful tune and a dove flew to his side. He took out a piece of parchment and began to write a message. He tied it to the back of the dove, whispered to the bird, and it took off into the sky.

"To whom is the message delivered to?" asked Nick.

"To Sama, Nicolas. Our next destination is to Dasmerl. I asked him to meet us there."

"Dasmerl?" questioned Wilson. "That is where the Galinds were born. We ran away from there a long time ago to look for our father. That's when we were taken as slaves. It would be wonderful to see home again."

"And it means good luck for me, as well," said Merdoc. "I will see Sama again."

He looked at the pendent around his finger.

"This is our friendship pendent. There's never been a bond like this before from a warlock and a dragon. Sama took care of me when I first hatched out of my own egg. That was when dragons were becoming extinct from Hermalie."

"Aren't most of them dead?" asked Arlene.

"As a matter of fact," said Merdoc. "the dragon population did begin to grow. Sadly demons started hunting us then. And now we are back to being endangered. Dracsen and I were the last ones. Now Dracsen is gone and...AAAHHHH !!! I'M THE LAST DRAGON!!!...Oh, how life is so rough! And all I ever wanted was a girlfriend. Oh, woes me!"

Darwin snickered behind his hand and Arlene hit him on the shoulder.

"Don't lose hope, Merdoc," said Arlene. "You'd never know. Maybe there is a girl dragon out there. And she would love to be with you."

"That would be nice. But it can't happen considering the fact that I'M-THE-LAST-ONE!"

"How pathetic," said Darwin softly.

The party stopped in the middle of Hermalie Field.

"Are you ready, Merdoc?" said Rozin.

"Ready for what?"

"For your training. Can't have a dragon in battle that can't fly or breath fire. I saw what happened to you back at the cave."

"I showed courage," said Merdoc with pride.

"Yeah, and you......FELL...for it?" said Darwin.

Merdoc growled.

"Watch it, shrimp!"

"Focus, Merdoc!" boomed Rozin. "Follow my instructions. First you have to run as fast as you can. Once you think that you have enough air, flap those wings of yours, and let them lift you into the sky."

"Ok! I can do this!"

Merdoc began to run.

"I can do this! I can do this!" he chanted.

He jumped off the ground and began to flap his wings. Then he started flying into the air.

"I'm doing it! I'm doing it! I'm flying! I'm flying! I'm......I'm falling! I'm falling! May day! May day! Incoming! I'm gong down!!!"

The group on the ground quickly moved out of the way. Merdoc landed on his head and fell flat on his stomach.

"Umm....not bad," said Rozin. "We'll work on keeping you off the ground later. Let's move on."

Merdoc rubbed his head and stood back up.

"Now, to breath fire, you have to take in a deep breath. Once you feel the air in your lungs become hot, blow!"

Merdoc nodded. He took in a lot of air. He held his breath and then blew out. But it wasn't fire that came out. Clouds of black smoke circled his head. Merdoc began to cough.

"Did I...did I mention that I wasn't always a smoker?"

*   *   *

They made it to Dasmerl before the sun began to set.

"Wait here, Merdoc," said Rozin. "we'll look for Sama. It'd be best if we didn't start chaos in this town. We'll let you know when we find him."

"Understandable," said Merdoc with a frown.

The rest of them began to walk into the town. They moved towards the entrance until a man, dressed in colorful clothes, put his hand in front of the.

"Halt!" he demanded. "What is your purpose in Dasmerl?"

"We have a meeting here with a warlock. He goes by the name of Sama Harless," said Rozin.

"And what is the purpose of this meeting, Sir Elf?"

"Of....reuniting...And to have a good time here in this wonderful town. We have heard so much about the gypsies and we wish to join them in their festivals."

The man looked at the party and back at Rozin.

"Accepted! Enjoy your time here, Sir Elf."

Rozin bowed and began to walk into the town. The man stopped him again.

"I almost forgot," he said. "before I can let you and your travel companions forward I must ask you to remove all weapons you and your party are carrying."

Rozin nodded and they all started removing their weapons. Arlene remembered what Sama said:

' *Keep this wherever you go. Never let it leave your sight.*'

"Goody Lady?" said the man. "Do you carry a weapon?"

"No," she lied. "I carry no weapon. I am just a woman."

"Very well. Carry on!"

And they entered the gypsy town.

*   *   *

There was so much life in Dasmerl. Music was playing by gypsy performers who entertained the crowds on the streets in tents. They were surrounded by crowds of people.

Stands were selling items and it looked like the gypsies couldn't wait to get their hands on one. Arlene saw two gypsy girls standing and admiring a gypsy man as he played the wooden guitar in the tent.

"He is so talented. And so dreamy!" said one of the girls.

"They're all like one, big, happy family," said Eron.

He then glanced to his side and saw two gypsy men fist-fighting.

"Umm…maybe not happy."

Arlene looked around.

"Where is William and Wilson?" she asked.

A cheer was heard. The group turned to the noise. Arlene saw William and Wilson on top of the crowd. The crowd was throwing them into the air and then catching them.

"Whooo! Hoo!" cheered William. "Arlene! Come join in the fun!"

"I find this to be nothing but absurd!" grunted Evensen. "Look at these people! They dance in a bizarre way, the music is a headache,and…."

"Hey, Sir Centaur, would you like to buy some fumar?"

He handed Evensen three white sticks. Evensen growled and the gypsy boy ran away in fear.

"Come on, Arlene!" said Darwin.

"I can't."

"Why?"

Arlene patted her side where the sword hid behind her cloak.

"Oh," Darwin walked away and joined William and Wilson.

"I want to join in this human activity!" said Eron as he followed behind Darwin.

"Rozin, any sight of Sama?" asked Evensen.

"I do not see him," he said as he looked at the crowd sharply with his brown Elf eyes.

"Good afternoon," said a man with red hair.

His clothes were colorful in red, white, and blue.

"I am Owen Porter. Leader of the gypsies. I welcome you to Dasmerl."

"I thank you for your greeting," said Rozin. "I am Rozin Whitestone. King of Lindolin City. This is Arlene and Nicholas Leggora. Prince and princess of Menellia. And this is Evensen."

"Nice to meet you, Sir Rozin, Sir Evensen, Sir Nicholas, and Goody Arlene."

Eron returned from the crowd of gypsies. He was sweaty and out of breath.

"Gypsies are like heathens!" he said. "They push, shove, and they lift me up just to drop me heard first!"

"I'm glad that you see it our way," said Evensen.

"This is my brother," introduced Rozin. "Eron Whitestone. Prince of Lindolin. Eron, this is Owen Porter. Head of Dasmerl."

The two bowed for each other. Eron was still trying to re-gain his breath.

"We are looking for Sama Harless. Have you see him?" asked Arlene.

"Harless....yes, as a matter of fact, I have seen him. Come, I will show you to him."

Owen led them to the tent where Sama waited. Darwin and the twins stayed with the crowd.

"Sama Harless?" called out Owen.

Sama walked forward with a smile.

"Oh, it's so good to see you all again!" he said with joy. "How's Merdoc?"

"Well," answered Rozin. "but we are having some difficulty."

"Difficulty?"

"Sama, he doesn't know how to fly or breath fire."

"Of course he does! I've seen him fly and breath fire."

"I do not think that he has the skill anymore."

Rozin brought Sama outside. He led the old warlock where he had last left the dragon. By the time they got there it was too late.

"Merdoc!" shouted Rozin. "What have you done!?"

Merdoc feasted on the gypsy cows. Their bones were stacked neatly next to Merdoc.

"Good Angels!" the dragon cried. "Now that was a meal!"

Sama laughed, "Merdoc, do you remember me?"

"How can I forget such a close friend. Hello, Sammy."

"Hello again, Merdoc. Tell me why did I hear from Rozin that you cannot fly or breath fire?"

"It's from being stuck in that stupid cave! I forgot everything. And now I have to fight this war."

"Speaking of war, Rozin, I've spoke with Owen Porter. He has agreed to fight on your side. At least now there is a part of the human race that will fight for our world."

"That is wonderful news, Sama," said Rozin. "But it is not my side. It is Arlene's side. The Seventh Angel is the true leader. Not me. I have faith in her."

"As do I," said Sama. "as do I."

* * *

Back in the town, Arlene stood alone. Gypsies danced to the music being played. The gypsy performer held his hands high and started moving his fingers rapidly in the air as he was dancing. The gypsies started mimicking him.

"Goody Arlene," said Owen. "Are you nervous?"

"Nervous?"

"About the war of Hermalie?"

"How do you know about that?"

"Sama Harless told me all about it."

Owen took a deep breath in and out and then he walked in front of the crowd. The music stopped and the gypsies looked up at their leader.

"My people, please listen to me! I must say this now and not later. There is war on Hermalie. And I have decided to join the side of the Seventh Angel. The king of Bensen Palace is dead. His son refuses to fight. I need every, single, healthy man to fight along side my warriors. I am sorry for this alarm. But our world is at risk of being destroyed."

The crowd was shocked.

"Gypsies?" questioned Evensen. "They are not capable of fighting! What was Sama thinking?"

"I don't know," was all Arlene could say.

"The gypsies are upset, "said Eron. "I fear the worst here."

Sama joined them.

"Sama!" shouted Evensen. "Gypsies can't fight! They have never fought before!"

"What is our choice, Evensen. The prince refuses. A

side of the human race is what we need."

"We need warriors! Not armatures!" argued the Centaur.

"Have you lost faith!? Speak to Hesion! You need the faith!"

Evensen stormed out of the group.

"Where are you going!?"

"To pray! These gypsies need it!"

One by one, Owen gathered men for the war.

"Please! Please!" begged a woman. "My husband has never fought in his life!"

"There is no choice," said Owen as he pulled the man out of the woman's grasp.

The men were led by Sama to a large hut.

"This is so sad," said Arlene. "I can't stand to see women and children crying."

"Yes, it is sad," agreed Nick. "But we all have to fight for freedom. Or else evil will take over us all."

"MURDERERS! MURDERERS!" screamed a woman.

She started throwing food at the party, but mainly Owen.

"If my son and husband die, you all will be labeled murderers! Murderers!"

Other women started joining in. And it was out of control.

"Quick! In here!"

Owen led them all into a small house. A riot of gypsy women surrounded, screamed, and banged on the small hut.

"Murderers! Murderers! Burn in the hands of Malenda! Murderers shall burn for the Queen of Hell tonight!"

*   *   *

Owen fed them and they all slept peacefully once the women were calm. Arlene dreamt about the war. There was dead humans, Elves, and Menellians. Dead demons, also. There was fire, rain, and mainly death. Arlene was dressed in her rags again. She felt as if she were no longer a princess. She was invisible to all the beings fighting. Except one. A cloaked figure stared at her. Arlene stared, too. Inside the figure's dark hood glowed a pair of red eyes.

"Arlene!" the figure said. "You will not live! You will die! You will fail! The Seventh Angel always fails!"

"No! You lie!" yelled Arlene.

"You will fall! You are scared of failing!"

"I am not afraid!" lied Arlene.

"You doubt your feelings!!"

"No!! Stop!!"

Arlene covered her ears.

"I'm not scared! I'm not scared!"

"You are pathetic!" yelled the figure. "You will die!! you will rot!!"

"NO!!"

Arlene felt the sword in her hand magically. She looked up at the blade and then at the figure.

"I'm not afraid!" she yelled. "I am not afraid! I will not fail!"

She charged at the figure but then the figure disappeared.

"Can you make it through tonight?" the figure's voice said through the wind.

Arlene smelled smoke and she began to cough.

"Arlene!" yelled Darwin. "Arlene! Wake up!"

Arlene opened her eyes. Rozin, Nick, Owen, the twins and Eron used their blankets to put out the flames. Half of the hut was on fire.

"Arlene, help us!" begged William.

Arlene got up, grabbed her blanket, and tried to put out the flames. The fire was spreading.

"We have to escape!" cried Nick.

He ran to the front door but he couldn't open it. William tried to open the back door.

"They're stuck!" cried William.

"The women nailed the doors shut!" cried Rozin. "IS there another way out?"

"There isn't!" confessed Owen.

"Damn it all!" shouted Nick.

Nick raised his hands. The door was shaking. Some of the nails were becoming loose from the outside of the door. Then a fireball headed straight to Nick .It hit his hands and he screamed in pain. Arlene rushed to his side.

"What happened?" she asked.

"Magic and fire have a connection of strong forces of earth. So they attract." said Nick in pain. "I wanted to risk it."

The fire was taking over. The women were cheering outside of the hut. Then they started screaming. A growl was heard over the flames.

"It's Merdoc!" said Eron.

Water poured onto the hut. Arlene shield Nick as it poured in. After the water, Sama knocked down the burned door.

"C'mon! Get out!"

The party began to run out of the hut. Merdoc was too

busy intimidating the crowd of gypsy women. Arlene looked up and saw her aunt flying on a broomstick.

"Aunt Harmony!" she shrieked.

Aunt Harmony lowered her sword after the last drip of water dropped from the blade.

Owen looked at his people.

"I place you all under house arrest! Guards, take them away!"

Gypsy guards started seizing the women.

*   *   *

Arlene sat outside with a cup of tea in her hands. Her wet clothes were off and she was in a gypsy dress. Eron took off his shirt and started ringing it out. Rozin and Harmony helped Nick with his burned hands.

"I will not fail. I will not fail." Arlene started saying to herself.

Eron couldn't help but hear what she was talking about.

"That is what you said in your sleep. What happened?"

"It said I would fail, Eron. I was scared. I was believing what it was telling me. But I had the sword in my hand when I didn't realize. I felt strong. Right there I had faith. I wasn't scared. Now I am not scared. I feel it. I feel the courage I have been trying to find, Eron. Now I know I am ready. I am ready for anything."

"Arlene?" called Harmony.

"Yes, Aunt Harmony?"

"Come here, child."

Arlene lifted herself up and walked over to her aunt.

"Keep your eyes focused tomorrow, and keep your head clear of anything negative. She knows about you, Arlene," said Harmony.

"Who?"

"Raven, the cloaked being."

"That was Raven? How did you know about my dream?"

"Nick isn't the only one who can read minds. I want you to be safe. Raven is a foul Menellian. And very powerful.

"Aunt Harmony?" questioned Arlene. "Why was Raven banished?"

"Before you were born, Raven was practicing the dark arts in Menellia. Such practices were forbidden but she did it in secret. The Onyx family learned with her. Their goal was to overthrow the Leggoras from the crown. My grandfather found out about their practices. The Onyx family blamed Raven for controlling their minds and made them practice the dark arts. They claimed Raven wanted them as her personal servants.

"The story was believed by the people and Raven was banished. Now Raven is after the Leggoras and the Onyx family. But Onyx is too petrified to stand up to Raven after their lying performance."

"What would happen if the Onyx family didn't lie?"

"They'd be banished to Forbidden Island like Raven. But thank the angels that they did lie, Arlene. They would be as powerful as Raven."

Arlene could imagine Demetra being powerful.

'*As evil as she is,*' she thought. '*but what about Piper?*'

*   *   *

The women in the huts were screaming and cursing.

"Shut up!" yelled a guard as he banged on the door. The men woke up from their slumbers and investigated on the noise.

"What is going on here?" asked one of them.

"The women attacked the travelers and Porter," said a guard. "They are under house arrest."

"Please, let us speak with them. Just to make the matters better."

Owen admitted the men to speak with their wives.

"This is going to cost me," said Owen sadly. "now my people hate me."

*   *   *

The party gathered their belongings and they rode their unicorns to Lindolin City.

"Arlene, we are fighting tomorrow, "whispered William. "What if we do not survive?"

"Don't say that, William," said Arlene with a sad tone in her voice.

"Arlene, we are no different then the gypsies. I was born in Dasmerl. Being that I was only a child, and I do not know much about those times, but I do know what they are feeling. It's despair disguised as anger. Arlene, there are times when I wish that you didn't pick up that sword."

"Be grateful, William .If I didn't find the sword we'd be dead. We would burn with the others in Alexandrite. Then Hermalie would burn in Hell. William, there are risks in life we all have to face. All we have to do is believe. No, we cannot think about failing now. This is what Raven and Malenda want. They want us to be scared. They want us to think that we are worthless. Nothing but slaves with swords. We're not slaves anymore. We are warriors and the angels have faith in us. We should have that same attitude, also."

"Arlene Leggora, I have always admired you. You were always smart. And I wouldn't expect more from a best friend."

"Nor would I, William, for you. Nor would I."

"Shh!" interrupted Rozin.

"What is it?" asked Darwin.

Rozin perked up his Elf ears and looked all over the field. The party drew their swords from the sheaths quietly. Eron spoke quietly to Rozin in their native language. Things were quiet and nothing was stirring. But Rozin refused to let them go any further.

"I ain't afraid of no demon," said Merdoc proudly.

A large growl flowed in the wind and Merdoc began to shake.

"Rozin…Rozin…" whispered the dragon. "let's make a break for it."

"Shh!" hushed Rozin.

There were loud bangs that made the earth shake. And they seemed to get louder, and louder, and louder.

"An ambush!" cried Rozin.

In front of them came a small army of demons and gargoyles flew in the sky. And on the back of a black unicorn was Xander himself.

"Get the Seventh Angel! Leave her unharmed. Do whatever you want with the rest of them!"

"Prepare for battle! Guard Arlene!" commanded the Elf king.

The party charged at the monsters. For once, Arlene was not afraid. Feeling the slash of the blade to a demon's flesh, she never felt braver.

"For Hermalie!" she shouted.

Nikita charged in and began to trample the demons to the ground. Harmony chanted and bolts of magic flew from the tip of her sword at gargoyles. Merdoc lowered his neck and started using his teeth to chomp on demons.

"Eww! You all taste like licorice!"

Xander made his way to Arlene. The black unicorn was as fast as the wind.

"You will not touch her!"

Nick stepped in front of Xander's unicorn. Liberty whinnied in intimidation.

"Foolish thing you are, Nicholas Leggora. Tell me, would you sell your own soul to Malenda for her?"

"I will die for her!" said Nick as he raised his blade into the air.

"You'd die in vain! Your sister and yourself will join a grave with you mother and father. My mother will rid the Leggora scum! Let's see how you bleed, hero!"

Nick and Xander's sword collided into each other. And then magic flew like lightning bolts out of the tips of their blades. Xander didn't aim for Nick anymore, but decided to aim for Liberty. Liberty was struck in the leg. He fell and he took Nick down with him.

"Excuse me, young prince," said Xander sarcastically. "my mother waits for her gift."

Xander rode towards Arlene. Sama couldn't stop him with magic, for Xander somehow blocked it before he could let out a spark from his wand.

"Arlene! Run!" shouted the warlock.

Arlene tried to turn Nikita around but Nikita wouldn't move.

"Come on, Nikita! Come on!"

It was like Nikita was frozen in her place. Xander rushed up and grabbed Arlene from her unicorn.

"Arlene!" shouted Eron.

He tried rushing to her aid but couldn't because the demons were blocking him. The party had lost the battle. Xander's unicorn rode off into the night and then into the big black sky. The Seventh Angel was captured. What will happen now?

~CHAPTER 10
A BLOODY BATTLE~

"Retreat! Retreat!" shouted Rozin. "To Lindolin! Quickly!"

"No!" denied Nick. "I cannot leave Liberty!"

"The unicorn is on his way to death, boy!" said Rozin. "you must leave him!"

"Go, Nick!" shouted Harmony. "Leave Liberty with me!"

Harmony lifted her arms and chanted. A flash of yellow light gleamed from her sword. The gargoyles and demons shield their eyes and then turned to stone.

"Nick, over here!"

Merdoc was patting his back. Nick got onto the dragon,and held on tight as Merdoc ran through the grass.They fled to Lindolin City.

*   *   *

The weary group stayed inside the castle and began to rest. Their minds were on Arlene.

"Arlene is the key to saving this world. If she dies there will be an end to Hermalie. The Seventh Angel will no longer exist." explained Sama.

Gloria poured them all a fresh cup of tea. They sat quietly in the Elvish castle and pondered on what will happen.

"This is my fault," Nick shook his head while he was looking down at the ground. "I failed my sister. There I was, thinking that I was able to protect her. Now…" He took a moment pause. "Now Raven has her."

"Nick Leggora," started Eron. "This isn't over until we declare it over. Back there, that was just a lost battle. But I swear to the angels that put me on this world, put the blood in my veins, and my sword in my hand, Hermalie will rise above Malenda. Hermalie will stand beautifully, Hermalie will concur her ups and downs. And Arlene, the heart of Hermalie, will now and forever never give up. We all love Arlene. I know we do. A hero is someone who makes the impossible possible. A hero saves. But what happens what the hero needs saving? The ones that love her are always there. Let's fight tomorrow. For Arlene and for Hermalie!"

"Let's think," said Merdoc from outside the window. "There will be a possible death for us all. Hell will take over, just maybe. Maybe even dragon stew for demons…Let's do this! Yeah! I'm up for another adventure!"

Merdoc began to sing.

"Forbidden Island, we go! Forbidden Island, we go! High-ho the dar-y-o! Forbidden Island, we go!"

*   *   *

The black unicorn arrived at the dark castle. The gates then closed behind it. Xander took Arlene off the unicorn. Her mouth was covered with a black cloth, her hands were bound behind her, and the sword laid in the sheath on her side. Xander dragged Arlene until they arrived into a darkened room. The room with the cauldron and the candles lined up neatly and lit. He threw her in front of him and started untying the cloth that wrapped around her mouth.

"Welcome, Arlene," said Xander. "to the castle of Malenda."

The room gave a chill down her spine. Arlene was silent. She was too scared to speak. She stared at Xander as he was looking through the spell book. He started adding herbs and other materials to the big black cauldron.Bat blood, dead weeds, demon skin, human skin, the toe of a dragon, slug guts, and others that made Arlene feel nauseated.

"Are you going to kill me?" she said when she finally worked up her courage to talk.

"Well of course, Arlene," said Xander. "We cannot have the Seventh Angel interfering with our plan. Malenda wouldn't like that. Once you are dead, Miss Leggora, the passing of the Seventh Angel dies, too. There will no longer be a heroine. And everything in Hermalie, the field, the Elf city, the gypsy town, the palaces of the humans, and you kingdom of Menellia, will all belong to the Angel of death and chaos.

"My mother will rule Menellia. It has always been her dream. Your aunt, brother, those Onyx traitors, and all the other Menellians will be calling her queen.

"But you, Arlene, you will be a shadow in the darkness. There you will lay in your grave, covered with black roses, as the Seventh Angel. A failure to Hermalie."

He walked to her and gently stroked her cheek. Arlene started hating him more than anything.

"How do you like that fantasy?"

Arlene gave him dirty looked and spat in his face.

"It's as ugly as you!"

Xander wiped the spit from his eye. He looked at her, without any emotion, and then drew his dagger to her neck.

"You don't know who you are dealing with!" he threatened. "If you want to live long enough to see your friends again, I suggest you be a good little girl!"

Now Arlene showed no fear. She didn't care now if Xander killed her or not. At least it would end the madness for her. Xander moved Arlene's cloak from her side. He stared at the sword's handle.

"I'll get rid of this junk first!"

He pulled the sword away from Arlene. Then the handle started turning into a bright red color. Xander's mouth dropped and he began to scream. He used his free hand to grip his right wrist. He couldn't let go of the sword. He fell to his knees and the sword was getting hotter in his hand. He found the strength to let go of the sword and he was still screaming in pain. He ran over to a small fountain in the room and stuck his hand into the water. Steam rose from the water and it made a hissing sound. Xander gazed at the sword with evil eyes. He grabbed a glove and put it over his burnt hand. He picked the sword up and the handle was glowing red again.

Even through the glove, Xander could feel the burning of the handle. He ran over to the cauldron and tried to shove the sword into the potion. The sword bounced out of his hand, made a bright flash of purple, and fell to the floor. He made three more attempts to destroy the sword, but it bounced out of the cauldron, with a flash of purple, and fell to the stone floor. It was still beautiful as it was the first time Arlene saw it.

"Impossible!" yelled Xander.

He removed the burned glove and walked up to the spell book. He thumbed through the pages until he found the page that told the story of the Sword of the Seventh Angel.

"The Sword of the Seventh Angel," he read out loud. "Created by the five Heavenly Angels. It was brought onto Hermalie to protect the world from the powers of Malenda. Only a brave heart can yield the power of the swo...I know that! Why can't I touch it!?"

He turned the page and read the words.

"The sword is an ally to all who are unskilled, or show an objection to black magic. The sword cannot be touched by any sort of evil. Such as wizards or witches that possess dark magic, demons, vampires, or any creatures from Hell. Others include dark beings such as dragons or mermaids."

Now Arlene knew why the mermaids feared the sword.

"The sword is indestructible. Magic and fire is not stronger, or more powerful, then the sword itself. The Sword of the Seventh Angel is the only truest, most feared immortal in the history of Hermalie."

*   *   *

The people of Hermalie wasted no time that night. They prepared for battle and marched to the Forbidden Island. Humans, Menellians, Elves, and Dwarf-Elves, covered in armor and carried weapons, boarded the ship and took off into the sea. Eron stood at the front of the ship. He sang quietly to himself:

"Let's fight for our happily ever after.
For all the things in life that matter.
One touch of hope is all we need.
A happily ever after for you and me."

Rozin, Gloria, and Trevis from Lindolin broke into the song when Eron got to the third line.

"What's the matter, Eron," asked Gloria.

"I'm worried about Arlene, "he admitted. "I am praying to the Angels that she is still alive."

Gloria looked at her armor, her sword, and then to the direction of the Forbidden Island. (Which looked like a black dot now on the horizon.)

"This reminds me about mother and father. And the soldier we saved years ago."

The three Elf men listened to what she had to say.

"Our mother and father were brave. And now we stand on their ship and we sail to save Hermalie. They are looking down on us, brothers and friend. They are smiling. I know it. If we die, let's die for our people."

*   *   *

Evensen practiced his battle standards with his staff. Sama practiced magic with his wand. Evensen stopped and looked out into the horizon.

"The sea is always blue. The sky, also. Hermalie is home and I'd hate to see it destroyed."

"Someday it will all disappear, Evensen," said Sama.

"I'd rather see it many years from now. Not today."

*   *   *

William, Wilson, and Darwin sat by themselves. They looked at the warriors.

"I feel out of place," said Wilson. "I'm so nervous. I've never fought in a war before."

"We all haven't. I know that. But it is not the war that is on my mind now," said Darwin. "What if that Xander character kills her? What if he already did?"

"Don't think about that," said William. "She'll be ok."

"Now remember what I said," said Harmony. "vengeance leads to evil."

"I understand, Aunt Harmony," said Nick as he put his sword back in the sheath. "but I hate Xander! And I swear to the Heavens, if he does anything to Arlene, I will not turn my back."

"I admire you, Nick," said Merdoc. "You have a strong heart, lad. If I were ten years younger I'd be as brave as you. I lost my touch years ago."

"Why?"

"Little man, you weren't the one who was unconscious back at the cave."

"Alright, alright. Let's start now."

"Start what?"

"Your training. You've got to breath fire."

"Fine."

Merdoc drew in some air.

"No! No!" said Nick.

He pointed away from the ship.

"That way! That way!"

Merdoc turned his head and he blew out the air. Sparks started to shoot out of his mouth.

"Ok, not bad," lied Nick.

*　　*　　*

Arlene sat at the huge table inside the dark castle. Xander sat beside her.

"You must be hungry."

He handed her a plate of food. Arlene frowned when she looked at it. She was in fact hungry. But she didn't know if the food was poisoned. She wanted to live a little longer.

"I'm not touching it," she said.

"What are you afraid of?"

"This food is poisoned."

"Well aren't we the psychic. No, it is not poisoned. Orders by my mother. I am not allowed to kill you. Not yet. Mother would slice my head off if she found your corps on this very floor before she got a glimpse of the Seventh Angel's eyes."

"What does she want with me?"

"You'll find out soon enough!! Now eat something!!"

"This is probably part of some ritual! If there is

something that she wants from me! And on how you want me to eat so badly!"

"Fine! Starve! I do not care!"

He threw the plate on the ground and Arlene jumped. He turned his back on her and he was quiet. He stared at the painting on the walls of his mother, Raven Darkshadow.

"You don't love her, do you?" she asked.

Xander's focus was on her now.

"What did you say, girl!"

"You…you do not love her, do you?"

Xander gave her a glare. The same glare that her uncle would give her when she asked a question. It always made her feel that she never should have asked.

"What makes you say that?"

"By the way you say 'mother', by the way you talk about her. It sounds like you don't love her. You don't care for her. Almost as if you despise her."

"I don't love," he admitted. "I only hate. I hate so I can survive. There isn't any love in this world. No matter how hard you look! The world is a dark place! I serve for evil! Do not question me about love, Arlene Leggora!! It does not exist in my world!!!"

He turned and walked away. Arlene felt the tears swell up in her eyes. Then Xander stopped in his tracks.

"It's here," he said. "the war has began. It's for Hermalie. It's for you."

*　　*　　*

Gargoyles and demons waited for the people of Hermalie to arrive at the island.

"Take down all in your path!" instructed Rozin. "Leave none alive!"

Owen started shaking.

"Never did I think that I would go through something like this, Sir Rozin," he said. "now my courage is as dark and lost as this land here."

"Do it for your people, Sir Owen Porter. Your courage will be kindled then."

The gypsy men were scared, too. Some began to cry as they held items that belonged to their families. One man clutched a lock of hair from he wife while another man held a ragged doll from a daughter. Gargoyles flew through the air, demons cheered as though they have already won the war. The men started sweating in fear.

"Do not fear them!" commanded Rozin. "Fear is death! Let them fear you!"

The ship boarded the island and they all jumped onto the ground.

"Charge!" shouted the Elves.

The armies collided into each other. Merdoc jumped off the ship and he made the island shake. He used his gigantic hands and feet to smash the demons under him.

"Die, Hell scum!" he shouted. "Muahahaha!"

Gargoyles started to gnaw on his wings.

"This will teach you not to bite!"

Merdoc pushed his wings back and it knocked the gargoyles into the sea. Magic was flying from tips of daggers and swords from Menellians. Elves were fast with swords. The Dwarf-Elves rushed in and attacked demon by demon. They tripped them with rope and they'd get together to plunge their daggers into the demon's skin like a pack of wolves to it's prey. Gloria,

Eron. and Rozin fought side-by-side together. Darwin and the twins did the same.

" 'ello, o'chap!" called a voice from under Darwin. Darwin slays a demon and looked down at his legs. There stood Benjamin Goldfeather.

"Benjamin! Didn't expect to see you here," said Darwin.

"Nor did I, Mr. Galind."

Darwin took down another demon.

"You're well with a sword," said the little Elf. "and so am I."

Benjamin jumped high into the air and flipped over a demon. He was a great fighter. The little Dwarf-Elf took one monster down by himself. Benjamin whipped the black blood off of his tiny sword with a handkerchief.

"All right! Go Benjamin!" cheered the twins.

Evensen and Sama worked together on a group of monsters.

"Evensen! Look out!"

Evensen turned. There were a group of demons holding torches. Sama drew his sword. He laid his wand next to it. He chanted and a strike of lightning glided against the blade. The bolt started to split and it struck the demons. The lightning lit up the battlefield. The torches fell and fire began to spread.

"Stay away from the flames!" commanded Rozin.

Menellians, Elves, and humans began to die. The land was flowing with fire, bodies, and red and black blood. Arrows were flying in the air by the Menellians and Elves.

*   *   *

No one in Hermalie has ever stood on the Forbidden Island. And there, in the place where everyone feared to stand on, it was known as the greatest and most deadly battle ever fought in the world.

"Aunt Harmony!" shouted Nick. "This battle will continue, not unless Raven or Arlene dies. I have to save her!"

"Nick, I want you to be careful."

"Don't worry. I have been trained well. And I promise vengeance will not overpower me."

Nick took a hard look at his aunt. As if it would be his last. He fought his way to the castle, ready to save Arlene.

"My people!" yelled Rozin. "Attack the gate!"

A line of demons stood on the castle gate. They had gigantic bowls of lava carried on their backs. Arrows of the good were too late to stop them. The lava was poured onto the people of Hermalie. Nick paused as the lava was poured from the gate wall. He spotted a rope dangling from the entrance and he used that to swing himself from the lava on the ground. Meanwhile Eron was outnumbered. He was weak and tired as he fell to the ground. The demons raised their swords over their heads and they were ready to kill. Then Rozin and Gloria rushed in to his aid. Eron got up from the ground but then fell down again. His leg was gashed and he was in pain. A demon stared at Eron and held his sword over him.

"No!" screamed Rozin.

He ran over to help Eron and stuck the sword into the demon's heart. The monster paused and took his last look at the King of the Elves. He took his hand and ripped off Rozin's chest armor clean. He drew his sword right into Rozin's heart. Eron felt Rozin's blood drip onto his face. Gloria's mouth dropped. The demon fell to the ground along with Rozin. Eron limped to Rozin's side. Gloria on the other.

"Rozin! Rozin!" shrieked Eron. "Oh, Rozin. Forgive me, please."

"What for, Eron," said Rozin softly as he held his bloody chest. "I did what I had to do. I had to save...the king."

"No! Don't say that, Rozin!"

Gloria began to cry.

"Hold on for us, Rozin," she begged. "we're going to help you. We're going to get you out of here."

"Save Hermalie, Glorifia. The only place that I will go to is the Heavens. Arlene needs your help. She...she is...th...the...chosen one. Be brave fo...for me. Fo...for our people. I love...I...I love..."

Rozin couldn't get his words out. He looked at his sister and brother for the last time and closed his eyes forever. Gloria and Eron mourned with their heads together.

"You can't leave, Rozin," cried Eron. "we need you."

William, Wilson, and Darwin saw the dead Rozin. Their eyes lit up with anger and they clutched their swords with tight grips. They screamed and killed every demon that came their way.

"For Rozin!" shouted William.

The Elf warriors looked at their dead king. Trevis raised his sword in the air.

"For the king!"

The Elves roared in anger and shouted their battle cries. Demons began to retreat but the Elves didn't allow that to happen.

Merdoc continued to stomp on demons.

"For the king! For the king!" he cried.

The enemies started to shoot arrows at him. Merdoc moved his face out of the way and he started to flap his wings. Then he started to lift into the air.

"I'm flying?"

He looked at his feat and saw that he was off the ground.

"I can fly! I can fly!"

Fire started to come out of his mouth.

"I can blow fire!"

Merdoc landed his eyes on the tiny demons and gargoyles. He smiled an evil smile and rubbed his fist with his other hand.

"Ha! Ha! Die!"

He began to fly and blow out fire.

"Run!"

The demons began to run for cover.

"I am the Almighty Merdoc! Feel my wrath!"

Fire started to shoot from his nose.

"Who's your dragon?"

*   *   *

Owen was circled by gargoyles.

"He looks tasty!" said one of them.

"I call his gut!" said another.

"No, you maggot! That's mine!"

"Go to Hell!"

The gargoyles stated fighting. Owen just shrugged and then walked away.

*   *   *

Nick made his way into the castle.

"Kirlana, protect me," he prayed. "and I pray Arlene is still alive."

*   *   *

"Do you feel it?" asked Xander.

"I feel nothing," said Arlene.

"Hermalie is dieing."

"Liar."

"No, I am not lying. One of your friends have fallen. Tisk, tisk."

She threw herself onto him and started banging her fists on his chest. He pushed her back onto the floor.

"I do not believe you! You lie!"

*   *   *

Nick found himself in a dark room.

"Spooky….spooky," he whispered.

Someone grabbed his shoulder. He turned and that is when he saw Raven Darkshadow. He could tell it was her even though her face was covered by the shadows.

"Nicholas Leggora, looking for your sister? How sweet! You're just in time to join a grave with her."

"You will fall, Raven, I swear!" said Nick in boiling anger.

"I beg to differ."

*   *   *

"I'm not afraid anymore, Xander," said Arlene. "I have been blessed by Kirlana. She has shown me bravery. Nothing you say now will change my mind."

"Arlene, the Angels are blind. I can't touch the sword, but you can. You are right, Arlene. You are brave. You are strong. You are more powerful than the last two Angels. Think of what you can do? With the sword in your hand you can concur all. You're stronger than the Angels. Join us, Arlene."

"You're pathetic, Xander. More pathetic than me back when we were fighting at the castle. I'd rather die a thousand deaths than to betray my people, my family, friends, Hermalie, and the Angels of Heaven."

"Be careful what you wish for. You might get it!"

The doors burst open and Raven Darkshadow entered the room with her hood over her head.

"Arlene Leggora, I have been waiting for this moment for such a long time."

"Raven Darkshadow," said Arlene.

"I've brought a wandering puppy, Xander."

She threw Nick into the room.

"Nick!" cheered Arlene.

But Nick wasn't himself. He looked dazed and ill.

"Nick?"

Arlene walked over and touched his arm. A jolt of a tiny lightning zapped her fingertips. She let out a tiny scream and nursed her fingers.

"What did you do to him??"

"He's my pet now," smiled Raven.

~CHAPTER 11
THE CLOAKED WOMAN~

Nick stood beside Raven as he was staring at Arlene.

"Nick, it's me. It's me, Arlene. Nick, please say something."

"He doesn't understand," said Raven. "he only responds to me."

"You got what you wanted, Raven. I am here. Please, let my brother go."

"I've been running out of servants, Leggora. You're brother is strong and handsome. He's perfect."

"Him?" argued Xander. "He's the one I want to bleed dry more than anyone in this world. He is useless!"

"Hush!" hissed Raven. "Or I will bleed you dry by cutting off your careless tongue!"

Xander's anger began to rise. Nick looked down at the floor and he was unaware of what was going on.

"The first to die will be the Menellians," began Raven.

"I'll rid the backstabbing Onyx family nice and slowly. How stupid can one family get? They thought they could be more powerful than me. I cannot wait until I see them beg for mercy!"

"As much as I hate an Onyx myself, I will not let you destroy Menellia! Nor Hermalie. Twenty three years ago, you tried to look for me. You tried to kill me before I could find the sword!"

"And I killed your parents for it, too. I know the story, Leggora!"

Arlene's eyes lit up.

"So you did kill my parents!"

"Your parents refused to tell me where you disappeared to. For that, they paid the penalty of death. And here you are, Arlene Leggora. Right in the castle of my Angel."

"I am not scared."

"Then I guess that I have to put the fear back into you. Slave, the girl!"

Nick threw his head up and was immediately obeying Raven's orders. His eyes glowed as tiny lightning bolts glided across his iris. He walked closer to Arlene, and Arlene began to step away.

"Nick! It's me! Arlene! You're twin sister!"

Nick ignored her calling and continued to follow Raven's words.

"Do not listen to her and do as I say!"

Nick grabbed Arlene's arm and her body began to light up as she was being shocked by his touch. She screamed in pain until Raven told him to let go. Arlene collapsed to the ground and clutched her stomach.

"It's sad...don't you think, Raven," she said. "you

need others…to do your dirty work for you."

"Are you challenging me, Leggora," questioned Raven.

Arlene was silent.

"Then a challenge is what you'll get."

"Let me do the honors, mother," offered Xander.

Arlene was confused.

"Honor for what?" she asked.

Raven waved her hand in the air, as if to tell Xander it was ok, and Xander grabbed Arlene and held her tight.

"What is going on?" she demanded as she tried to struggle out of Xander's death grip.

"Arlene Leggora, I am Raven Darkshadow and I have never lost a challenge. Before my victim's death I put a symbol of my victory on their body."

Xander tilted Arlene's head to her right shoulder and moved her hair away from her neck. Raven took the end of her blade and started carving the symbol into Arlene's skin.

Arlene started groaning in pain as she felt the sharp tip dig into her skin.

"Nick!" she yelled. "Nick, please help! Please help me!"

Nick still stood there looking down at the floor. He was still under Raven's spell. Raven removed the tip from Arlene's neck. The blood spilled from the wound. It was shaped like an arrow. At the tip of the arrow head were flames that were now covered in Arlene's blood. The wound began to burn like fire and soon enough her neck felt like the flames of the arrow would take over her. Blood was flowing like a waterfall. And it seemed like it would flow forever.

"Now, Leggora, pick up your sword and fight me 'til your death."

Arlene began to look back at her past. From being a slave for her aunt and uncle, the slave party to the riot, meeting the royal family of the Elves, falling in love for the first time, finding her long-lost family, and here she is now putting her life on the line for a better future. A future for the people of Hermalie. For all that has happened in her life twenty three years ago she knew she came from a long way. Another back flash appeared in her mind. Back at her aunt's stable.

'I'm going to escape, Darwin," her voice echoed through her head. *"I'm going to explore Hermalie. I want to see the Elves. I want to meet Menellians. I want to have an adventure! I want to go down in history!'*

"I got my wishes!" she said out loud.

Xander and Raven began to study her words.

"I got what I wanted! I got my dreams!"

"What are you rambling about?" demanded Raven. "Stop daydreaming and fight me, you weak little maggot!"

The fire in Arlene's eyes began to burn as she looked up at Raven. She picked herself up and walked over to her sword. She reached down and gripped the handle with her right hand. The sword began to glow. And Arlene knew she wasn't going to die. Not now. Because of the sword, her dreams came true. It's takes a miracle, like the sword, to make a slave into a hero. And some courage is what Arlene needed in this point of her life. Arlene walked in front of Raven and pointed the tip of the Sword of the Seventh Angel at her.

"If it's a fight you want, Darkshadow, so be it."

"About time!"

Raven's blade against Arlene's made an evil hissing-like noise and it echoed throughout the room. Xander rushed over to Nick and pulled him away from the fight. He dragged him to another side of the room and then pulled out his dagger. Raven ended the fight by pushing Arlene out of the way. She grinded her teeth together when her eyes saw Xander with the dagger.

"What do you think you are doing with my slave, boy!"

Xander stopped what he was doing.

"You don't need a Leggora to be a slave, mother. He's useless!"

"You are not the judge of that! I demand you to let him go!"

Raven stormed after him.

"Oh for the hatred of Malenda, mother, an enemy is not an ally! I suggest someone else. The vampires are better servants than him and the good-for-nothing demons that run around this island!"

"I maybe your mother, but I am also queen of this island! You will obey my orders! And I say I want the Menellian prince!!!"

Raven and Xander continued to argue and Arlene decided to run away with Nick. She snuck quietly over to him while the other two were too distracted. Nick's eyes were closed and he stood still behind Xander. She reached over and touched Nick's arm with her index finger. A spark shot at her finger and it made her jerk back. She took her sword and laced the end of the blade around his cloak. She began to pull him backwards and he began to follow.

'That's it, Nick. Come on," she said with her lips moving and without a word escaping from her mouth.

Arlene brought herself and her brother to a shaded area behind a bookshelf. She made sure Raven and Xander were still arguing. Then she turned her attention back to Nick.

"Nick! Come on, Nick! You have to fight the curse. It's me, Nick! It's Arlene!"

Nick slowly opened his eyes and looked into hers.

"That's right, Nick," she said smiling. "It's me, Arlene. Come on! Snap out of it!"

Nick grabbed Arlene's neck and he began to choke her. Small lightning bolts glided across his eyes and Arlene's body began to light up. Raven and Xander stopped arguing and turned to the light behind the bookshelf. They rushed over and saw Nick with Arlene in his grasp.

"He's the perfect servant," said Raven as she smiled a half smile. "if ever I see your dagger in him, I swear to Malenda my sword will pierce you!"

Xander felt the rage of hate and anger build up inside of him.

"Congratulations, mother. May a Leggora be more trustworthy than myself."

He stormed out of the room. Arlene felt the life being sucked out of her as she was being tortured by Nick's touch. The sword laid by her feet and that is when it clicked to her.

No evil can touch the sword. And Nick was cursed in evil.

"Stop with the slow torture, slave! Finish her off!!"

Arlene never wanted to hurt Nick. She loved him

dearly and just the thought of it pained her inside more than the torture she was going through now. But Arlene had to put that all aside. She reached down and picked it up. She pressed the handle onto Nick's face and the sword began to glow the bright red. Nick's face began to release smoke and he screamed. His shocking touch began to die down and his grip on her neck was loose. Nick fell to his knees with his hands covering his face. Arlene continued to bring in the air to her lungs as she stared down at her brother. He was still screaming and he threw himself onto Arlene. His hand was on the sword but the sword did not glow. And it didn't hurt Nick in any way. Arlene held onto Nick and she laid the sword next to her.

"Nick? Nick, look at me."

Nick raised his head and revealed the side of his burned face,

"Arlene....Arlene....:

"Nick, I am so sorry."

"Don't....I am so sorry. You saved us both."

"Leggora, Leggora! Prince and princess. Sister and brother. Together again. This is a real touching scene, if you ask me," said Raven sarcastically. "As touching as the day you two were born. I saw your father trying to protect your mother from me and they worked so hard to keep the Seventh Angel from my power. But now I see that their death will be in vain due to the fact that you're both standing in front of me right now. And I am sick of this pointless chit-chat. So let's get on with the dark magic, shall we?"

Raven's magic shot out from her fingertips and Arlene Nick moved out of the way. Arlene fell onto the bookshelf and caused it to fall. Glass bottles smashed and books scattered all over the floor.

"You cannot run from me, Arlene!"

Red lightning bolts appeared as Arlene tried to run away. Nick's hands were raised in the air and fire leaped onto Raven. She screamed and tried to put out the flames on her cloak.

"Arlene, run out of the castle and get onto the ship. Take all survivors back to Hermalie!"

"I'm not leaving you here!"

Nick picked up her sword and tossed it to her.

"Arlene, leave!"

"Nick, our parents died because of her! We never knew them because of her! And because of her, twenty three years of my life was sold to slavery! She has stolen everything from me and I'm getting it back!"

"Vengeance is a sin, Arlene!"

"Nick, let's skip the rules just once and take the vengeance we deserve!"

Raven got back onto the feet and her burned skin began to heal. Her cloak was mended together again in the sharp red color. She turned and discovered that Arlene and Nick were no longer standing behind her. The twins hid in the shadows once again. Only this time they were invisible. Arlene couldn't see Nick and he couldn't see her. Now she understood why the color of the clothes they were wearing were for protection. The colors made them invisible in the dark.

"Who came up with this idea for Menellians?" she whispered.

"Father did," said Nick." Ever since, Menellians have been known for stalking well in the dark. It's magic.

Black is our cultural color .Now shh! She'll hear us."

Raven walked passed their hiding spot.

"Arlene, take this."

A green dagger floated in the air.

"We're ending this. This dagger belonged to mother. This one here," a back dagger then floated in front of Arlene. "belonged to father. These daggers will not finish her off. But it is for mother and father. Use your sword to end her life."

Arlene understood. The two walked out of their hiding spot and quietly walked behind Raven.

"Foolish children," she said. "are you afraid of me?"

"Are you kidding?" said Nick

He twirled her around and stuck the black dagger through her breast.

"That was for father!"

Arlene followed.

"That was for mother!"

Raven gasped in pain and then straightened herself. The daggers pulled themselves out of her body and fell to the floor with clings.

"Idiots," she said. "you cannot kill me! I am the truest immortal!"

She began to laugh her devilish laugh. Arlene held up the Sword of the Seventh Angel.

"And this is for us!"

Arlene plunged the sword into Raven and Raven began to scream. The sword began to turn red. Arlene pulled it out and returned it back into Raven's black heart.

"This is for my stolen twenty three years!"

Arlene continued with the stabbing.

"This is for my family…this is for my suffering…this is for Hermalie…this is for King Edward…this is for…"

"Arlene! Stop!" yelled Nick. He pulled her away and Arlene pulled the sword clean from Raven. Raven fell dead to the ground and black smoke rose from her body.

"Revenge is a deadly sin, Arlene. It can corrupt anyone's mind. The last thing we need is the Seventh Angel turning to the evil side. Do not leave our side."

Arlene began to calm down.

"I promise. Cross my heart and hope to die."

Nick smiled and he brought her into his arms and hugged her.

*　　*　　*

The battle on the Forbidden Island was over, and Raven Darkshadow was finally dead. Thanks to one brave warrior and this story that no one will ever forget. Returning back to Hermalie seemed like peace that Arlene had been longing for. For Owen Porter, it seemed he had a battle to fight back at Dasmerl.

"He's dead!" shouted a gypsy woman. "My husband is dead! Curse you, Porter! Curse you!"

Many women were reunited with their men. But the unlucky ones had their fingers pointed at Owen.

"They died with bravery," said Owen to the crowd of gypsies. "They fought for a future for yourselves, your children, and your children's children. You do have the right to mourn their death, but think of all the wonderful things that they have done for Hermalie? Goody Arlene and her companions believe in the well being of our future. Your men followed the same courage. As do I. To the surviving men, you are now looked upon as heroes. To the men who lost their lives, they are heroes, as well. And may we never forget them. And for them I have declared that statues are to be made in their honor. And in your family's honor."

Some women cried, same with the heroes,and yet some were angry. Arlene knew what Owen was trying to say.

"Goody Leggora, "Owen said as he bowed to her." I am in your service. I am in the service of Hermalie. Whatever you need in the future, know that I am here."

"And I ask you for one thing, Owen. And that is to comfort your people. No one lets the death of a loved one slide. Trust me. I know."

"Aye, my lady."

Owen bowed and said farewell to them all. Arlene, Eron, and Gloria walked out of the town.

"I miss Rozin," admitted Arlene. "and I never got a chance to say goodbye."

"This happen for a reason. At times I hate it. Like this time."

Eron's tears fell from his eyes.

"I do not want the crown."

"Eron, you must take the crown. You are now King," said Gloria.

Arlene was surprised.

"Eron, that is what your brother would want. He would want you to further protect your people. To carry on the royal Whitestone name."

Arlene took him by the hand.

"It's because he believes in you, Eron. I believe in you. As much as I love you."

Eron was in comfort by her words. He kissed her like it was the very first time. Gloria smiled and began to sing in her native language. A breeze started to pick up and it made her looked up.

"Look!" she said pointing to the sky. It was Merdoc and on his back was Sama.

"Merdoc! You can fly?" asked Arlene

"Yeah! And, Arlene? You were right!" cheered Merdoc.

"Right about what?"

"You were right about a girl dragon! Arlene, I have a girlfriend!"

Another dragon hovered beside Merdoc. She was pretty for a dragon.

"Everyone, meet Mercedis. Mercedis, this is the Seventh Angel."

"It is a pleasure, Angel number Seven."

She touched the ground and the dragon bowed. Arlene did, too. Sama jumped off Merdoc's back.

"Arlene Leggora, how do you feel about your courage now?"

"My courage?" questioned Arlene. "My courage is so high the Angels can see it in heaven. I can't wait for my next adventure."

The old man chuckled and Arlene giggled. She ran to Sama and wrapped her arms around his neck.

"And you've always seemed like a father to me. Thank you."

William, Wilson, and Darwin rode on their unicorns. They jumped off and they quickly embraced her in their arms.

"It seems like forever since we saw you," said Wilson.

"No, not forever, Will. Forever is a long time. I knew I'd see you all again. Come now, my friends. Let's go home."

~CHAPTER 12
ARLENE S GIFT~

In the night of Lindolin City the Elves gathered in the streets holding candles in their hands. Rozin's body laid on bundles of wood and he was covered with an elegant green cloak.

"I'll miss you, Rozin," said Arlene as she touched his face.

She moved back and stood between Harmony and Nick. Nick wiped a tear away from his eye, where he now has a scare going down his face in a crooked line. Trevis started singing as he took the torch in his hand to the wood. The fire lit up the faces of the mourning Elves. And Rozin began to turn to ashes.

"Why could you save him?" whimpered Arlene."Why couldn't you save him, like you did for me?"

"He was killed by the blade of steel. You were killed by the blade of black magic. Black magic is not a calling from Heaven. You see, Arlene, it was Rozin's time to go. The Angels called for him. He did what he had to do here on

Hermalie."

"Death is horrible. Everyone is in pain," said Arlene sadly.

"Death is a way of life, Arlene," said Harmony. "Death is nothing more, or nothing less, than the circle of life."

Arlene sighed as she watched the fire.

*   *   *

The next day Arlene headed to the ruins of Alexandrite. The town looked exactly like her past. Dark, bleak, and dead. Darwin and the twins were by her side.

"I cannot believe how quiet it is here all of a sudden," said Wilson. "the streets use to be crowded with people. And there was joy and laughter."

"Oh, Wilson. That only came from the rich folk," said Darwin. "this is nothing but a memory of the dark side of our lives. We've got Menellia now. And Arlene. Let's leave all this behind and begin for our new future of happiness. That is what mother and father would want for us."

"Of course, Darwin," said Arlene. "We've got the future that slaves in Alexandrite longed for. Our dreams came true."

Arlene paused and then walked up to the ruined Leggora home. It seemed like yesterday she was climbing out of her attic window to join the slave party. She looked down and spotted her old diary. She picked it up. It was half burned. She opened it to her last entry and read it out loud. It was the night her adventure began. She looked around again and saw a pendent buried under the ashes. It was Aunt Mary's Leggora Pendent.

She picked it up, wiped the dirt from it, and put it around her neck. William got onto his unicorn first when Arlene returned.

"I don't know about you but I want to head home," he said. "and by the way, Arlene, back at Menellia there is a surprise for you that I think you need to see."

* * *

The four heroes rode away from Alexandrite like knights back to Menellia. When they arrived Darwin and the twins guided her to Harmony. Harmony held in her hands a wooden box.

"Here she is, your majesty," said Darwin.

"Arlene, I want you to have this. It belonged to your mother and I wish to pass it onto you."

"What is it, Aunt Harmony?"

Harmony opened the box and revealed a shiny well decorated crown.

"It's beautiful!" said Arlene in awe.

Harmony sat the crown on Arlene's head.

"You look like your mother," she smiled and so did Arlene.

Then Harmony got a look at Arlene's neck.

"Arlene, you have been marked by Malenda's symbol!"

Arlene quickly covered it with her hand. Ever since it was their own secret to all that witnessed that moment.

* * *

Arlene walked out of the castle to take a breath of fresh spring air.

"Arlene Leggora!" shouted someone.

Arlene rolled her eyes when she discovered it was Demetra.

"I heard you defeated Raven Darkshadow. I highly doubt it! A slave like you defeating a powerful witch like her?"

"At least you wont have to worry about her coming after you family, the Onyx traitors!" Arlene said in a sarcastic tone.

The people started to laugh on the streets.

"So you've become a smart mouth, huh princess. Come! I challenge you, Arlene!"

Nick walked out of the castle and shook his head.

"Here, teach that Onyx a lesson."

He handed Arlene the Sword of the Seventh Angel.

'You think I should challenge her?"

"Yes, just tame her a bit. She is getting on my nerves!"

"Do me a favor and hold this for me?"

Arlene took off her crown and gave it to Nick. Menellians circled Demetra and Arlene as they began to fight.

"Have I ever mentioned, Demetra," began Arlene as they dueled." all those braids in you hair make you look really odd?"

Demetra grinded her teeth and started fighting a little harder.

"I once knew a slave in Alexandrite who had the same hair style as you. You look like her, too. Are you sure you didn't have a twin?"

"You're going to regret saying that, princess."

Demetra fought harder. Arlene was having no problem making Demetra's life miserable.

"Princess? I thought I was a bloody backed floor scrubber. Very strange how you call me slave but then call me princess on the side."

Demetra became angry and Arlene figured out her weakness. Demetra is evil so she looks to vengeance. Arlene didn't want to hurt the foolish girl so she just tripped Demetra with the blade.

"Demetra, you don't want to depend on vengeance. And you don't want to know how I killed Raven."

Topenga and other girls rushed over and helped Demetra off the ground. Arlene turned on her heals and walked away. But then a flash of green light flew across her face and it hit Demetra. She flew backwards and hit the ground again. The Menellians on the streets began to laugh. Arlene turned her head from the crowd and saw Nick lowering his arms.

"Why did you do that?"

"Hey, Arlene, I had to do something before she did. I saw the look in her eyes. Now I want to present you with my gift to you."

Nick brought her to the broom closet and opened it.

"I got you a broom."

He handed her the new broom.

"I was wondering, do you want a lesson now?"

"Why not?"

Nick grabbed his broom and they headed to the courtyard in the back of the city. Nick mounted his broom and then Arlene did.

"Ok ready? Do you remember everything that I taught you so far?"

"Yes I do."

"Are you nervous?"

"I'll let you be the judge of that."

Arlene had a big grin on her face.

"Ok, on the count of three we'll say the magic word together. One...two..."

"Ves!" shouted Arlene.

She flew high into the sky.

"Catch me if you can!" she laughed.

Nick said to himself: "I guess I have to train her in patients, too."

He looked up at her in the sky and fear spread across his face.

"Whooo! Hoo!" cheered Arlene.

"Arlene! Arlene! You don't know how to fly that well !You're going too fast!"

He flew into the Menellian sky and hoped to catch her.

"Oh please, Arlene," he said to himself again. "don't do anything stupid!"

~THE END~

THE LAND OF THE HEAVENS

~Character Information~

The Angels:

Kirlana: The youngest and the head Angel. She is the Goddess of Hermalie.
Zeles: Angel of Life
Afelle: Angel of Love
Hesion: Angel of Faith
Falari: Angel of Mercy
Malenda: Angel of Death and Chaos

The Leggora Family:

Arlene Leggora:
Age:22-23
Birthday: January 13
Sign: Capricorn
Race; Menellian/human
Description: Long brown haired girl, pale faced; went from rags to royalty; The Seventh Angel.

Nicholas Leggora:
Age:22-23
Birthday: January 13
Sign: Capricorn
Race; Menellian/human
Description: A dark haired male that stays with the traditional color of Menellians' clothes, black, a protection color; pale faced handsome prince.

Harmony Leggora:
Age: 42 (She was 19 when Arlene and Nick were born)
Birthday: September 4
Sign: Virgo
Race; Menellian/human
Description: A blonde haired queen and she is said to be the most beautiful being in Hermalie.

Anthony Leggora:
He is pale faced and dark haired like most Menellians. But he has the bitter side of humans.

Mary Leggora:
To Arlene's eyes, Aunt Mary had the beauty of a princess. Inside she was as ugly as a demon.
Kathryn Leggora (deceased):
Arlene and Nick's mother.
Daniel Leggora (deceased):
Arlene and Nick's father.

The Galind Brothers:

Darwin Galind:
Age: 24
Birthday: August 16
Sign: Leo
Race; human
Description: Light haired male, peach skin; from slave to warrior.

William and Wilson Galind:
Ages: 25
Birthday: June 16
Sign: Gemini
Race; humans
Description: Blonde haired males; they are funny and they love to pull pranks; from slaves to warriors.

The Whitestone Family:

Rozin Whitestone:
Age: 2,123
Birthday: February 10
Sign: Aquarius
Race; Elf
Description: He can be stubborn at times but he is also very caring.

Eron Whitestone (Name pronounced like the common name"Aaron"):
Age: 2,120
Birthday: December 3
Sign: Sagittarius
Race; Elf
Description: A true romantic Elf prince.

Glorifia "Gloria" Whitestone:
Age: 2,119
Birthday: April 14
Sign: Aries
Race; Elf
Description: A beautiful Elf princess; a wise and kind lady; is well respected.

Companions:

Merdoc:
Race; dragon
Description: dark green colored dragon with yellow eyes. He sometimes talks too much or acts a little strange but, then again, the nicest dragon anyone will ever meet.

Evensen:
Race; Centaur
Description: he has red hair and his horse body is covered in white, like a unicorn.

Sama Harless:
Race; warlock
Description: an old man with white beard and "stupid clothes" so says Merdoc.

Villains of Hermalie:

Raven Darkshadow:
Age: 43
Birthday: November 14
Sign: Scorpio
Race; Menellian
Description: She is an evil witch with long black hair and bony fingers with cat-like claws. Said to be the only immortal Menellian.

Xander Darkshadow:
Age: 23
Birthday: July 20
Sign: Cancer
Race; Unknown. Raven might have just created him.
Description: His personality is just like his mothers. He has the power of dream leaping and he is a necromancer. (conjuring the dead.)

Demons and Gargoyles: Servants of Malenda and Raven
The Mermaids: Beautiful beings that are selfish and know everything about Hermalie.
Dracsen: A powerful evil dragon; Malenda's "pet"

Onyx and Jade

Demetra Onyx:
Age: 22
Birthday: November 9
Sign: Scorpio
Race; Menellian
Description: She has a full head of braids and she looks like a pale evil Elf.

Topenga Jade:
Age: 21
Birthday: July 17
Sign: Cancer
Race; Menellian
Description: A light haired Menellian. She is Demetra's friend and she is known to be an instigator.

Mother and Father Onyx:
The parents to Demetra and Piper Onyx

Other Characters:

Trevis: A close friend to the Whitestone Family.
Owen Porter: Head of the gypsies.
Benjamin Goldfeather: A Dwarf-Elf
Rupert Goldfeather: Benjamin's son.
Josephine: One of the elf children that watched over Arlene.
Piper Onyx: The sister of Demetra Onyx; the only Onyx with goodness.

King Edward Bensen: Ruler of the human race.

Prince Thomas Bensen: A bitter prince; the favorite son of King Edward.

Princess Miranda Guenvil: A bitter princess who hates Elves; engaged to Prince Thomas.

Visit Danielle's website :
http://www.geocities.com/seventhangelonline

Printed in the United States
47138LVS00002B/46